D0338775

CIRCLE

NINE

CIRCLE NINE

ANNE HELTZEL

CANDLEWICK PRESS

Copyright © 2011 by Anne Heltzel

First edition 2011

Library of Congress Cataloging-in-Publication Data

Heltzel, Anne.

Circle nine / Anne Heltzel. — 1st ed.

p.   cm.

Summary: For seventeen-year-old Abby, the mysterious Sam is her sole companion and her whole life, but although life in his cave-palace seems ideal, she begins to remember her past identity and to question Sam's devotion in the face of an ever-changing reality.

ISBN 978-0-7636-5333-0

[1. Identity—Fiction. 2. Survival—Fiction. 3. Science fiction.]   I. Title.

PZ7.H3762Cir 2011

[Fic]—dc22   2010040148

11 12 13 14 15 16 BVG 10 9 8 7 6 5 4 3 2 1

Printed in Berryville, VA, U.S.A.

This book was typeset in Adobe Caslon, Dante, and News Gothic.

Candlewick Press
99 Dover Street
Somerville, Massachusetts 02144

visit us at www.candlewick.com

*For my mom, who taught me to
read books and to love them*

That Night

The rain falls around me in torrents, flowing from the mouth of the cave above us to the ground by my feet like a waterfall, splashing up at my toes. I am barefoot. I stand behind the sheet of water and let it mist around me, wetting my face and clothing. Its cold beads touch my skin all over like a thousand tiny needles. The rain has been like this all day. Sam is curled up on the metal cot behind me. Water drips through the ceiling on and around him. He's shivering, feverish. His body has turned a pale color, and his skin is nearly translucent. I never thought his skin, dark and rich like latte, could become this color, as if his anger drained it of its pigment. It is damp and unpleasant in the cave — so strange and different — but in a moment it may be incandescent and lovely again as always. Everything is distorted in my head, and I don't know which reality I'll wake up to anymore. For now, the air smells of mildew, and the walls leave a slimy residue on my fingertips when I make the mistake of touching them. We have Sam's cot and a folded-up blanket for me on the floor, and our clothes. We have run out of food, and Sam is needing his medicine more than ever. I think maybe his medicine is slowly killing him. But I know he's dead without it.

Even the rats seem afraid. They've long since stopped scuttling away. Instead, they huddle in the corners at night like they are on our side and we are all on the same level in this place. It isn't always like this. If everything was always like this, I don't know how I would live. I would never have come here if this, this confusing dark world, had always shown itself right along with the one I love and have grown accustomed to. I can't control the reality I see. I can't control what happens in my head. It used to be bright, beautiful, and full of life here all the time. I used to be happy here all the time. But that was before I started losing him, before I knew how he lied, before I discovered the Secret. I think that might be the trouble about disaster: maybe by the time it settles on you, you're already in the eye of the storm, and you don't realize what's happening until it's already done. Maybe that's what has happened to us. I only wish I could think clearly, see things clearly, the same way every time.

I walk over to the fire I made earlier this morning— it is struggling, fighting to stay lit against the damp. I warm rainwater over it for tea. No tea leaves, just warm water, enough to pretend; and after all, I am used to pretending. I laugh at this bitterly. I put a cup of my makeshift tea to Sam's lips, hoping it will warm him. Our cups are dirty tin, and a few plastic ones we've collected over time. As much as I am angry with Sam, I hate to see him suffer. Nevertheless, my fist tenses around the cup until I can gauge his reaction.

Abby? Sam whispers. He is delirious but gentle. *Abby, don't leave me. Please don't leave me.*

That is what he is most afraid of, what he's been afraid of for weeks since I've started figuring things out. He's fought to hide every shred of the truth from me, but I have still managed to piece some of it together, and it's left him terrified. It wasn't always this way. There was a time when the world began and ended with Sam, and we were happier than I could have imagined would be possible. Now he senses my pity. It is the most powerful emotion I can remember feeling in months. We both know something is about to happen. We are waiting for it, dreading it and wanting it all the same.

PART ONE
SLEEPING

CHAPTER ONE

Fourteen Weeks Before

I wake up and there is a boulder in my skull and a hand on my cheek. I startle and struggle to lift myself from the ground, and when I do, bolts of pain stab my eyes and brain. I lie back down. I let the hand caress my cheek, because it's the only good thing I feel right now, and I want to hang on to it.

In the seconds that follow, I assess my surroundings. I am lying in an alley. Or maybe a small, empty lot between two houses. The air is saturated with the smell of cinder and meat, as if there has been a giant cookout nearby. I turn my neck cautiously and feel it creak, hot-poker pain shooting up my head and down my back. I can barely make out the feeling of intense heat, then the flames to my left, which blaze a strange, brilliant white against the last of what looks like it had once been a two-story home. Then I turn to my right and see an angel-god-boy. His face fills my line of vision, infiltrates my nerves and synapses until the hairs on my body rise toward him and my heart strains against my rib cage.

Come with me, he says urgently. His eyes are molten lava. He looks over his shoulder and takes my hands in his. *Hurry,* he tells me. *They'll be coming soon.* I hesitate at first, and he tugs my wrist hard. *They'll come to put it out.*

Put what out?

This fire, he says impatiently, looking behind me.

I turn and stare at the rubble through the smoke haze. I'm sure I've never seen the house before. Just to make certain, I look long at the yard, at the houses beyond. I've never seen any of them before. I've never seen this boy before, either; I am sure of it until just after I've thought it, when nothing seems sure at all.

I know you? I ask. A few seconds tick by, and he stares hard.

Yes, he says carefully, speaking slower than before. *You know me.* His eyes look confused, like he can't believe I'd forget.

I let his words sit there in my head until they feel comfortable. The boy looks sweaty, panicked. His eyes dart to one side and then the other, a metronome of glances. He looks afraid. For me?

My eyes move to the striped tank top I'm wearing, then the tattered jeans, both heavy with soot. I don't recognize these clothes. Something thick lurches in my gut. Would I recognize my face if I saw it?

Come on, he says again, his voice so tense it might snap.

Who am I? I whisper. His face is a mask of confusion, and mine is only a mask.

Who are you?

I nod. There is a pause. His eyes dart downward and linger there for a moment, like he's trying to figure out how to handle me. Like I'm an unpredictable thing.

You're Abby, he says, meeting my eyes again.

Abby? I ask him. The name rolls thick and unfamiliar off my tongue.

Yes, he says, and his confidence and urgency have returned. *It's written right here.*

He taps my chest and I flinch, but he's only going for a thin gold chain that encircles my neck. He gives it a quick tug. I look down and see there's a name formed from cursive gold, an upside-down *Abby.* Is that who I am? A girl who carefully selected this chain from all the rest, mulling first over rows of gold, cursive names?

He's tugging me again, harder now, saying something: *Abby, we really have to go right now. They'll be here soon. There were others in there.*

Where are they now?

They didn't make it.

Who are you? How do I know you? I am reluctant to leave.

Sam, he says in a gravelly, smoke-congested voice. *I'm your friend, Abby. Now, let's move.*

I nod slowly and a strange look passes over his face, something like pleasure mixed with relief. I remember Sam about as well as the house, but I let him help me stand up anyway and then I nearly collapse, I am coughing so hard. The boulder in my skull has turned into a knife. It halves my brain. Right brain, left brain—they are halved already anyway, so I'm not worried. Sam lifts me all the way up, draping me over his shoulders as if I'm a sack of feed and he is a mule. I press my cheek against his shoulder, where I can faintly feel his skin pulsing with exertion, and it *is* familiar somehow. I feel suddenly as if Sam is the only person I have ever known, and I don't even mind, because I hear distant voices and all of a sudden I have to leave as badly as he does. Something about all of this seems so desperately wrong.

We are silent for many minutes. My sharp panting sounds staccato against his longer, deeper breaths. I am glad to be on his back. I'm relieved he's taken charge. I wouldn't have known where to go on my own. No one is behind us; no one follows. It is just the two of us heading away from everything else.

For a time, I sleep.

Where are you taking me? I ask him when I wake in a fog after what seems like many hours.

North a few miles, he tells me. *Just up a ways into the forest, to my place. You'll be safe there.* I hear his breath laboring, shorter and quicker now, so I wriggle my way down his body. I am small, but not so small that carrying me miles would be easy. We go on like this for a while, me stumbling in halting steps and him leading. I have to stop a lot to catch my breath. It seems my lungs are full of something thick and unkind. My right arm shrieks in pain when I grasp Sam's elbow for support. And when I can't make it anymore on my own, he carries me again. And again I sleep.

When we get to Sam's, he puts me down on the ground. I am awake but barely—just enough to see that Sam doesn't have a house. He has something better: a craggy underground lair like a hidden kingdom. He brings me tea and plumps pillows on a mattress for me, then helps me up so I can nestle on it. The mattress is on the ground, like what you might find in Asia, but I'm not sure how I know that or whether it's accurate in the first place. I am suddenly seized by the compulsion to know who I am. I search for memories, but my mind is empty and there's a profound exhaustion settling into my limbs. I remember nothing and no one. I look at Sam drowsily and am at once so grateful to have someone by my side. I trust him. Then I realize it doesn't matter whether I do. I try to think about the right and wrong of this, but it eludes me. It's as if all of my innate senses have vanished entirely.

CHAPTER TWO
Fourteen Weeks Before

I try to be wary of him because I have to be. It's as if I've been built with some internal device that tells me to fight my instincts. This device is different from my instincts, and both are different from my heart. I don't know what to trust: my gut, my brain, or my heart. Which one speaks the truth? So I am wary because my head tells me to be, I am tempted because my heart has sought his ever since I opened my eyes and found his face, and I am inclined toward him because I know I have no other choice.

Besides, there was a certain gentleness about him last night. The way his face curved up in a tentative smile as if he were hoping I would like him. He asked questions with his body: His shoulders hunched up when he pointed to my bed. His head tilted to the side as he watched me sip my tea. He wants me to like him, and every little bit of insecurity betrays who he really is: someone I can trust. His other gestures, the hard ones — I know he's cultivated these the way I've cultivated my own. How do I know? Instinct. *Something*, something I don't quite remember, tells me to keep my distance this first full day. But the rest of me says that after today — after

I've told him in my own way that I, too (yes, even I who don't know my own name), come equipped with these senses—after that, after boundaries have been established, then I can relax.

I don't know my own name.

I think of this and search back in my memory for what must have once been there. But there is nothing. An empty void punctuated only by the same knife stabs I've felt for hours. The nothingness is oh-so-exhausting, my head so racked with pain, and I fight hard to keep my eyes open at the unbearable recognition of this awful chasm. Knowing nothing means there is nothing for me anymore, and as I look at him, I come back to the simple fact: even with the keenest instincts I have no choice. I must depend on someone. I stare at him, his dark lashes framing his still-sleeping cheeks. It could be much worse.

While Sam is sleeping and my headache abates, I assess my surroundings more carefully than I did last night. It appears we are in a cave, but it is like no cave I have ever seen. It's a palace carved from rock in the recesses of the ground, and sitting in it, I feel like Persephone. But this is not Hades; it is light and life. There I am again, trusting my instincts. It's much harder to trust my brain because when the brain is empty, I suppose it must create its own truth.

And so this is not so odd, this cave-palace. If it isn't Hades, then it is the opposite—paradise. For the walls shimmer gold and I see that Sam has decorated them with his own art: word art, which surely if carved away from these recesses would be fit for a distinguished gallery, it is so lovely. The rich blues and oranges and purples of phrases and poems glitter like the walls themselves, and suddenly I'm no longer Persephone but Hatshepsut. This beauty drifts into my head as easily as the air damp with morning chill that decorates my skin. My brain, in its spongy emptiness, is filled all at once with this beauty. Beauty restores me. These things are knowable to me — Hades and Hatshepsut — in the same way I've found other bits and pieces knowable over the last day, when I reach into the recesses of my brain. They rattle around in there, alone amid a bunch of space. The space is the important thing. The space is all the things I don't know. I know a million Otherthings, but what I *don't* know is who I am. So I let the beauty sink in deep, and I focus on the Otherthings, and I let it be a cold sponge to my searing fear.

Everything yesterday was disordered; everything today is more disordered still. I went to sleep last night and woke up today in a world infused with color and a mysterious boy to share it with. I woke up today with phlegmy coughs the color of tar and boils on my skin. I am light, I am happy, I am free. I am hurting, I am worried, I am lost.

I let it go. I focus on light, happy, free. I stare at my

blistered hand and watch it heal over as if by magic. It is magic; now I feel sure of it. I feel no pain. I rise above it; it cannot harm me here. I walk to the mouth of the cave, now my home, and look out all around me. I can see that it rests in a wilderness of sorts, and now I am neither Persephone nor Hatshepsut but Snow White. The world around me is early-morning damp. There is a blue lake, glistening; I am surprised it doesn't bore bright tunnels into my eyes. There are trees that strike green arrows into a clear sky. Everything is new and lovely. Fully restored, I retreat back into the thing I call paradise and wake my prince.

CHAPTER THREE

Fourteen Weeks Before

I am lounging on a gold damask sofa, my feet in Sam's lap, sipping pomegranate wine we made ourselves. The lighting is warm; it gives off colors like orange and yellow, not purple or blue. It envelops us like the goose-down comforter we keep on our bed.

The bed became "ours" from "Sam's" yesterday. It only took days. Am I the kind of girl that slips under someone's sheets after just a few short days? What is implicit in that kind of girl? What other things can you learn of her from that simple fact? But what does it matter; I don't know the rules anymore. It's freeing, anyway, to live moment to moment because you have to. When you have no past, when time and history don't matter, you can be mistress only of your present decisions. You can't even really look forward, because what would you base it on? Decisions you make today? Having no history, I decide, is a blessing. I wouldn't want to be cursed with the memory of a lifetime of mistakes.

Sammy is reading to me: Dante's *Inferno*, by Dante Alighieri. Another someone famous I've never heard of. I've not been here long, but it's enough to know that I know nothing about who I am or who anyone else is, except a few random bits of information floating around unfettered in that space I call my head. Sam can be my library, my just-beginning, hopefully never-ending well of interesting facts and startling truths. I've been alive three days; there was no life before this.

I levitate above not knowing. I transcend everything that came before.

I am blissfully happy. As Sam reads, I finger the notebook he keeps around, much of its contents torn out and scattered like rubbish through the cave. They're half-covered with bits of phrases and rambling sentences; I think how nice they'd look with pictures, too. What's left of the notebook feels right in my hands, as if it belongs there. With a pencil, it's complete, a natural part of me. But for now I'm just listening, holding the notebook and allowing Sam's words to drift over and around me. Sam is kneading my toes with his palm; my stomach is full with my last meal, which still lingers on my tongue. I stare at him staring at the tattered pages in his hands — the wear of the pages shows he's read this book more than once. I wonder why he loves it. I can already tell that Sam is a complicated person. I heard once, sometime long ago, that people are two types: uncomplicated or complicated. Cerebral or surface-level. I haven't figured out which type I am or which type I might like better. This book is hard to follow, but its jarring images stay with me. One man eats the back of another's head then wipes his mouth on the other man's bloody hair.

What do you see when you look around, Abby? I laugh at this; I am becoming used to Sam's games.

A circus clown on stilts, I say, all seriousness.

No, really. He jabs me hard in the arm, impatient. *Look around. Tell me what you see.* I see stone walls, etched with art like an ancient Egyptian tomb. I see the remains of a bountiful feast, goose and wine and fruits stacked a mile high: passion fruit, star fruit, fruits I've never seen before tonight. I see this gold lounge where we're reclining, and a faded red trunk in the corner, all shabby and antique. Our bed is canopied, and its mahogany frame is five feet tall. There is a tiny staircase next to it, three steps high, so we can climb up and collapse into its folds with ease. There's the other bed, my Asian pallet where I slept the first two nights, opposite us and barely visible in the second room. I relay all this to Sam, and he stares at me in wonder for a long time after I am finished. His reaction to my descriptions is startling; his eyes have begun to tear.

That's right, he whispers. *It's beautiful. You and me, our world . . . it's perfect.*

I nod in agreement. It's almost as if this thing we're living is a dream in reverse. The dreams I've had the past two nights have been jagged black. I don't remember them, but there have been trails of dried tears on my cheeks when I wake up. Dreams are supposed to be good, life a harsh reality; that's what I know from somewhere unidentified, knowledge lodged deep down from Before. My life with Sam is a rich tapestry, better than any dream state. My dreams are cursed. Everything has turned over on itself.

Then: *You should stay here always, Abby,* he says with eyes pleading. *You don't ever have to leave.* He looks frightened, like a child, as he says it; then in an instant he's back to normal Sam. I hug him closer, but what he asks of me is silly. How could I ever leave? Where would I go?

I focus on what Sam is reading; he's intensely involved in this story about the circles of hell and the people who are stuck there, condemned. The words roll over and around his tongue like a rich ice cream he takes time to savor.

O rabble, miscreated past all others,
there in the place of which it's hard to speak,
better if here you had been goats or sheep! . . .
But if my words are seed from which the fruit
is infamy for this betrayer whom
I gnaw, you'll see me speak and weep at once.

Betrayal. Fear. My head pounds, the knife resumes its merciless stabbing inside my brain. There is a sudden flash, a snapshot, and for an instant our underground palace lair is not a palace at all but a dirty, damp cave strewn with garbage and threadbare blankets and stained sheets. Then another flash and I blink and it is normal and lovely again. I shudder.

What, mija? Sam asks. *What is it, little girl?*

I saw a scary place, a place where everything is dark and ugly, I tell him. I snuggle deeper into his chest.

Not here, Abby. You and me have an invisible shield. We're protected from the ugliness as long as we're together.

Then, where?

Here, he says, shaking his book in the air. *And there.* He points beyond our cave lair. *It's out there,* he says, *that things are ugly.* He watches me carefully as if to gauge my reaction.

But I've seen it out there. The blue sky and glittery lake. They're beautiful.

Those are the lies, he says. *Those things ring false. Temptations that will betray you.* His voice is adamant, almost angry.

Like the ninth circle. I gesture toward the book, a catalog of hell. The ninth circle is the worst one, the part of the story I'm most afraid of.

Yes, just like that. His voice is softer now. I can see that he is pleased with me for making the connection. Then he leans closer to me, his face serious, and takes my hands gently in his. *That's where you were before, Abby. But you're safe now.*

Did someone hurt me in the ninth circle?

Sam pauses to think for a moment. *Everyone,* he finally says. *Everyone hurts everyone in Circle Nine, and they especially hurt you.*

Betrayal?

Betrayal everywhere. By people you thought you loved. It is hell out there. In here, we're safe. I saved you from it, remember? From the fire that night and from everything else out there, the horror of it.

And then I feel it. The splitting pain below my heart, a pain strong enough to match the one in my head, the thing I didn't feel the other day but I feel now in a panic. I am afraid of *something* I am concealing from myself. It will gut me if I dwell on it.

I can't go back there, I say to him. I shudder and push the darkness out, and I focus on the room around me, on our world and its comforts.

You won't go back, Sam promises me.

CHAPTER FOUR

Thirteen Weeks Before

Grease is everywhere, all over our beautiful stone floor. Sam spilled it there. He'd been making bacon and tipped the pan, and now the place is flooded. The glorious smell of bacon fills my nostrils but soon I realize I want to smell anything but bacon. Too much of something delicious becomes something poisonous. Sam's laughing at me; it's loud and full, and it carries over the sound of the pouring rain outside. I'm pretending to ignore him so he'll clean up the mess on his own.

Too good to help me, princess? Come on, baby. He hands me a rag. *Give me a hand.*

It's your problem, I say, wrinkling my nose. *You're the one who made the mess.*

Everything's us now, baby. We help each other out.

Sure, when it's convenient for you.

Don't be like that. He comes over and gently wraps his arms around me. Then he starts to draw me backward toward the soapy bucket he's prepared with the water that drips outside and sometimes inside, too, but I feel him falter and the bucket spills and his feet slide around on the floor and out from under him and he's clutching my shirt and then we're both on the floor, grease and sudsy water all over us.

Sammy! I yell. I turn my face to his. I try to keep it a mask of fury, but I can feel a giggle leaking out. Then he's laughing and I'm laughing, too, because everything about this boy is contagious.

Come on, he says. *I'll help you up.* I give him my hand and he pulls me up, but instead of letting me go, he's pulling me over the floor in a mad dash. I scream at him to stop, but his laughter kicks out my screams and replaces them with laughter of my own again. We run and we slide, first holding hands then separating when he gains more momentum than I, then we're on the floor again, rolling around in the stuff.

It's so much fun, my happiness is leaking out of me everywhere, pouring out of me and mixing with the water and bacon grease on the floor, which is mixing with my hair and my sweat. I see Sammy in a low crouch on the floor, the beginnings of getting up, but I jump up faster and tackle him back down. Sammy's skin is a special eau de toilette of Sam and pig. It should be disgusting, but it is delicious. I want to lick it. So I do. I lick his arm. He licks me back. I bite his lip. He bites mine. Then I taste his tongue, just to see. Then I'm enjoying the slippery-slide of his arms and his chest against mine.

Take a bath, Sam says after we're all tired out from being playful. *You stink.* I swat his arm.

What about you?

I have an errand.

An errand? It's not even night, I protest. Sam never lets me leave here except at night, even though he leaves often in the day. I pout. *Why should you get to leave all the time but you keep me here like a princess in a tower?* It is becoming a familiar argument.

Because I'm stronger than you are, he says. *I'm used to it.*

Please let me come with you, I say.

No way, princess. He pushes me aside.

That's fine, and he is strong, very strong, but I don't like it when he's not around. And sometimes I want to see more of the day. I go around in the woods just out-side our cave-palace, but sometimes I wonder what else there is. I reach back into the recesses of my brain and feel such a pang of fear when I do that I stop wondering and promise myself not to wonder anymore. Sam loves me and keeps me safe. Curiosity kills the cat.

Well, where are you going?

My business, mija.

No way, Sam. I shake my head sternly. *Everything's us now.*

You're right, he agrees, looking at me teasingly. *Who said that? Must've been somebody pretty smart.* Then he zips his jacket tighter.

Sam! I say. *Out with it.*

I'm just . . . sick, baby. Nothing to worry about, he says hastily because I must look as worried as I feel. *But I need to get something to help me out.*

Medicine?

Yes, I guess that's what medicine is, right? Something to make your body feel better.

So you're going to the doctor?

I'm going to my friend's, mija. *He gets it for me.*

OK, I say, but I am a little wounded. I don't know why I can't meet his friend.

Good-bye, little girl. He kisses me on the cheek, tells me not to look so sad.

I wait for hours until Sam comes back. I'm not sure what to do with myself, so I sketch. Sketching makes me feel somehow calmer, and I can tell by how good I am that I've been doing it for a long time, maybe years. By the time Sam comes back, I've nearly finished my sketch of a tiny cityscape, antlike people hurrying down the streets. I'm so happy to see him. I hug him right away, and he hugs me back, but he's much quieter than usual.

Something wrong, Sammy?

No. He smiles a big goofy grin and shakes his head. His eyes are shining, as if something wonderful lit them up from inside his head.

Did you bring us dinner? I ask. My stomach has been rumbling.

No. He shakes his head slowly and lies down on the

sofa. I'm a little disappointed until I remember that we have leftovers of a huge ham, the kind you eat at an elaborate feast, tucked away somewhere. I make us both a heaping plate of it with mashed potatoes, too, and we tuck up under the covers and eat in bed together. I ask Sam about his friend, whose name is Sid, and he tells me I didn't miss much.

I've got to keep you away from him, he teases. *He might like you a little too much, and then I'd be jealous.* I laugh, but his eyes look as if part of him is serious.

That's silly, Sam, I say. *I'm all yours.* We fall asleep together hand in hand under the covers with our plates littering the floor just until tomorrow.

CHAPTER FIVE
Thirteen Weeks Before

There are voices outside. Sam and I hear them at once. The feminine, lilting one and the other one, smokier and not as girlish. Our cave in the woods is the perfect little home. The only thing it lacks is neighbors. We are not used to hearing voices all the way out here. I sit upright in my chair, and quickly Sam is behind me, covering my mouth with his hand. I am perfectly still. I am not afraid, just curious. Sammy seems afraid, though. His hand grips my face so tight, and his fingers stretch in front of my nose, too, so it's hard to breathe. I snuffle a little until he relaxes his grip.

Shhhh, he whispers. *Not a sound.*

The voices grow louder. The girls are heading closer. Sam grabs my hand and we inch quietly toward the skylight, a rough-cut hole in the stone of the cave. It's as far as we can get from the sound of the voices. I can make out the words now. Sam pushes at the glass pane covering the hole, but it's stuck. I don't remember us ever opening it before.

What is *this place?* The girl with the pretty voice asks the question.

Just an old dump, the other one says. *Looks like an old mine shaft or something. Let's go.*

We pause. Maybe we don't need to go out through the skylight after all. Sam doesn't want these girls to see us. I feel like I don't want them seeing us, either. They're invading our little home. They're intruding.

Then we hear, *Let's just have a quick look around. Who knows? Maybe we'll find buried treasure,* and they're giggling and coming closer and Sam's tugging extra hard at the skylight and suddenly it grinds up and he's pushing my body through it. I'm struggling and I'm nearly halfway through and now there's silence.

Did you hear that?

What the hell was that?

Nothing. It was nothing. Come on, let's look.

Now I've pulled myself up to the grass, and Sam's after me, and he pushes the pane back over the gap almost all the way. We hear noises below us in our home.

Ewwww, the raspy girl says. *I told you it was just a dump. I'm probably getting some nasty disease just by standing here.* Her words slap me hard in the face. I am so proud of our lovely underground kingdom. Sam is clutching me hard again. I see him looking at me as the girl talks, like he knows I'm upset with her. My knees are pressing into the damp soil beneath me, and a tiny iridescent fly lands on my arm, but I don't swat it away. I must pretend as if I am carved from stone.

Jess, says the softer one, *someone's been here recently.*

Of course we have, I angrily retort in my head. Can't you see last night's meal in the fridge and our candlesticks on the dining table all covered in wax? Can't you see our rumpled sheets?

No way, the other one says, and I hear a note of fear in her voice. *This is totally freaky.*

Look at all this stuff on the walls, says the soft one. Her voice has wonder and fear in it, now.

Seriously, the other girl agrees. *If you want to stay, feel free. But I'm outta here.*

The other girl must want to join her because we hear their shuffling moving away again and the crunch of grass and twigs growing distant, then more distant, then gone altogether. Even so, Sammy makes me sit outside with him for a very long time. Finally he says we can go inside. I wonder what invisible messenger told him it was not OK for those other interminable minutes and OK at just this particular minute.

When we get inside, I sit at our long oak dining table, and Sam pours us coffee with milk. He sets my coffee in front of me along with a plate of toffee-butter cookies, my favorite, and a tray of caramels, his favorite, even though he says he buys them for me. My porcelain teacup has yellow elephants on it. I selected it myself. I know I did. But I can't remember when. I love my teacup and use it for everything, including coffee and juice. I fill it with water at night and leave it by my bed. I admire the way it looks smooth against the rough grain of our chop-block table. I gaze into its murky depths.

Abby! Sam's voice is harsh. He snaps his fingers in front of my face. *Focus,* he says. *We need to talk.*

What about? I ask, munching my cookie.

About what just happened.

I don't know what happened, I say.

OK, Sam says slowly.

I just think they were rude, I tell him after a minute. *They were not our guests. We did not invite them. They intruded and then they insulted us.*

That's right, he says. *They were just two very rude girls.*

And besides, I say, *our house is charming.* I take a long, trembling sip of my coffee. Something those girls said crept inside me and is nesting there. It wriggles around, making the rest of me feel uncomfortable. Why would they say these things that aren't true? Why am I threatened by these lies? I feel my head throbbing, my eyes wanting to water. The skin on my chin spasms, but I think the cup hides it from Sam. I am trying to be less emotional, and this is not helping. I want to show Sam that I am strong and he doesn't have to protect me all the time. Strong enough to leave here, sometimes.

The thing is, says Sam, *maybe they will come back.* I don't like this news at all.

Let's block the front. We could build a slab of something to cover it. It could be a makeshift gate. This is our place.

That's a good idea, he says carefully, *but it's even better if there's nothing. Because if we build a gate, they'll know we're here.*

Sam, how can anyone not know we're here! Is everyone so crazy?

I just don't want a gate. His voice is firm, the kind that means I can't challenge him and maybe I've already said too much. Then he relaxes a little.

I'm sure they won't be back. It's no big deal.

And if they do come back? And you're not here to look after me?

Just walk away and hide. Or if you can't hide, pretend you're like them, exploring the woods, too. Like you accidentally came across this place but you don't know anything about it.

Why can't people know we live here?

We're too young, Abby. We don't own this home. They might want us to go live with people in Circle Nine. I am horrified at this idea. *And then we'd be separated,* he continues, *and we might be in a really bad place, like a jail for people like us, people without families.*

That would of course be the worst thing that could ever happen, so I agree that if someone ever sees me here, I will pretend I am from the outside, finding this place for the first time and that I belong somewhere else. All so no one decides that they know best where we should belong. If I am ever separated from Sam, my life will be no more. I am not OK without him. I don't know of a life without him. It's like I was born with him and I plan on dying with him, too. I have trouble understanding my feelings toward Sam sometimes. It's not just as if he is someone who understands me. It is as if we were made from the same clay, and he *is* me. Our souls speak to each other all day long, and when they are conversationally at rest, they link arms. I have a hard time thinking of anyone else's soul even coming close to this with me. I think everyone else must be alien. So without Sam, I would be living among aliens, foreigners. I would be the only one of my kind. Without Sam, there is not me and anybody else. There is just me. Facing the world alone like that is the worst kind of pain I can imagine. It is not a possibility.

Even now he knows what I am thinking. He gently pulls my head to his shoulder and kisses the top of it, strokes the back. His hand pulls away all of my bad energy. With each stroke of his fingers on my hair, I feel him tugging out all the fear I've ever felt. When he is around, I can relax and let everything go. We spend the rest of the night playing chess, which Sam has taught me and I have taken to with remarkable skill. I have won seventy-two times, and he has won sixteen. By the time we are done, what happened before has blown through my mind, light and calm.

CHAPTER SIX

Twelve Weeks Before

Sam is out again. This makes twice in two days, which is highly unusual. I am sketching, but I sketch all the time and you can only pass so many hours filling up a blank page. But there's really no other choice, unless I take a nap. I have few ways to amuse myself when I am alone. I don't like to lose myself in my thoughts, because there's a limit to how far they will reach. For example, I can think of last night and Sam. Or last week and Sam. And my happy memories give me a good feeling, but it's no better than when he's with me in person, and when the memory-feelings fade, I realize he is not at my side and there's a crushing disappointment. So remembering good things often makes me feel worse in the end.

Or I can try to think of what happened Before. I simply don't if I can help it, because my mind is a blank void before that night, and when I push it further than it wants to be pushed, it retaliates by sending through me waves of pain and fear. I wonder if I feel the same pain and fear the people out there, who spend all their time in Circle Nine, do. Or maybe theirs is much worse than mine. I don't know how anyone with worse pain than mine could endure it. I think it's one of the things that makes me different from Sam. He says my sleep is rest-less. That I babble. That I wake him up at night.

My only other choice is to think of the future. This is the best way, but it's also difficult. My experiences that I can remember are so limited. That alley, that house. Sam, this cave-kingdom. Rumpelstiltskin and England in the Golden Age and Russia in the time of *War and Peace*. These last things are from the stories Sam's read to me and the stories that are lodged somewhere in my brain like flotsam I brought with me into this world. So I can imagine Sam and me living in a Russian palace, and I can imagine our behaviors and who we'd be, but we end up being exactly who we are now and doing what we do now except in a different, possibly more exotic kingdom than the one we live in. So that possibility is limiting.

When I am left alone, I think too much. So I sketch, because the effort it takes to concentrate on the page empties my brain. I have calluses on my index finger and that third finger, the middle one next to it. The one on the middle finger is hideously ugly and raised, a scaly bump. Some other marks on my right hand complement the calluses: angry red scars near my palm, stretching up to my wrist. Scars from incidents I don't remember. Together they form a red-and-pink mottled landscape. These, however, are my only physical flaws. I have exam-ined all the rest of me carefully enough to know that I am beautiful. In my opinion, Sam is as shockingly handsome as I am beautiful. Together, we must be blinding. That is probably another reason we go out mostly at night.

I am out of paper. Sam often brings me parcels of paper and fresh pencils, but he complains when I need more. I wonder if perhaps he has stowed more in his desk in order to make me think we are out and I must conserve. I wonder if it is a trick. I go to his desk. It is a rich, dark wood, possibly mahogany. It has an intricately carved pattern but only one drawer. I give the drawer a tug. It does not budge. I see a small brass lock blocking my way to my paper. I give another tug; the lock holds fast. I see a sharp object, a golden letter opener on the table and wedge it into the small space between the drawer and desk. It is encrusted with jewels. I use it like a lever and the drawer pops open.

There is only one thing inside, and it is not the loose paper I wanted to find. It's a small notepad instead, the same size and shape as a journal. I wonder if it is a gift Sam wants to surprise me with. I take it out. Now that I've found it anyway, I think it may not make a difference if I peek more. I take a closer look. I see right away that it can't be a new gift, because it's a little worn. I open it and the pages are drawn all over. I look at it again. There's something odd about it, as if I've seen it before.

Now my heart freezes into stiff stone, because I know.

The sketches covering the pages are mine.

The tentative lines, the detailed scenes, they're all mine.

I don't remember it.

It is something from Before.

Sam has been hiding from me this thing from Before.

My whole body turns cold. My fingers shake.

I take deep, long breaths for several minutes until I can breathe normally again. I close my eyes and wait for my body to stop trembling. I feel the compulsion to do *something*, but when I search my brain, I am at a loss for what action to take. Instead, I sit on the corner of our bed with the small journal clutched in my hand, waiting for him to come home. While I wait, I force myself to leaf through its thin pages, even as my head begins to pound. My panic does not subside, though what I find is innocent enough. Every page is filled; there are beach scenes, a few pages with characters that look like Sam and me. There are pages filled with fire, others brightened by glittering jewels. I see symbols of power—a crown and a scepter—on one page. And on another, a neglected garden, haunting and desolate. I don't see much joy on these pages, or purity, but there is hope in almost every scene. On one page, there is a river of tears rushing over drowning bodies, but one tiny figure in the corner emerges from the river unscathed.

I close my eyes and bring the little book to my face, breathing in its scent. I want so much for this artifact to bring me answers. It's unfair that I have nothing to make me whole, no past to form me into someone distinct. Maybe this sketch pad will give me clues. Maybe I will put myself back together little by little, starting now. I study each drawing carefully, scanning its details for some hidden message, something to conjure feelings or a memory. But I am still blank, other than what I imagine from the context: just some pretty work left over from a long, empty afternoon. Just some sketches I did to pass the time, like all the rest I do each day, nothing more. I can't help it; I begin to cry. I can't understand why Sam would keep this from me. What could it possibly mean to him? But to me it is a relic, the only remaining clue to who I once was. It was cruel for him to take that from me. It's been an hour, and he's still not home. It's enough time for my anger to boil up violently. I've never felt this anger toward Sam. I didn't know I was capable of feeling it.

I am sitting in the same place when Sam walks in. His look of happiness at seeing me changes into a quick flash of confusion and then something close to shock when he notices the object in my hand. For a moment I feel a heady sense of power. It is nice to catch him off guard, to be the one calling the shots. But then he switches on me.

I see you found it, he says offhandedly, taking off his coat and flopping down in an armchair. *Wish you wouldn't have gone through my things without asking me, though.*

He's whipped out a book and has already begun

turning its pages, as if this thing that's tortured me for an hour is a nonissue. I jump off the bed and walk right over to the chair and get in his face.

I was looking for paper, I seethe. And you had no right to keep this from me.

He raises one eyebrow and his mouth curls into a smile, as if he's amused.

Abby, he says, *you're being very cute. Why don't you ask me why I had it there?*

Why, then? I ask. I don't like his condescending tone.

Because you gave it to me to keep safe, he replies. *When you were lying there in the grass. Maybe you don't remember because you were still in shock at the time.*

What are you talking about? I say, and Sam sighs impatiently.

That day with the fire. You pulled this from your jeans and told me to keep it safe, that you didn't want to look at it but didn't want to lose it, either. So I did. I can't believe you don't remember.

I look at him carefully. His face looks open, like he isn't lying. And why would he lie to me? Sam's never been anything but good. And I have forgotten so many things. So why does something seem strange? Why are my fingers trembling? Why is my heart quickening in tempo with insistent protests of my brain? What is that buzzing in the back of my mind, as if there's something I need to realize, something big, something horrible?

Think, Abby. What do I want with it, anyway? It's just a pretty little thing; you've got loads more right here. He gestures to my recent sketches, the ones that litter our room like remnants, bits and pieces of rubbish that were overlooked. I think, and he's right. There's nothing in it he could possibly want. I take a few breaths and feel the anxiety slowly begin to diminish. I sink onto his lap.

I'm sorry, I say. I mean it. There is a comforting emptiness in the back of my brain.

That's OK, mija. *You just need to trust me. By the way, who knew you could be so dark? Some of that's all fire and brimstone.* He needles me in the ribs, then carefully lifts it from my hands. *It'll only upset you, babe. Let me throw it out.*

No! I shout.

Abby, Sam says. *These really mean nothing to you?*

No, nothing.

Then let me get rid of it. Look how angry and upset you are.

OK, I say, deciding he is right. Holding on to the object and staring at it and remembering nothing is more depressing than any of my futile efforts to search my mind for memories. Here is an object, actual evidence of my past, and I still can't remember a thing. It's hopeless. It's better to forget. It's right for Sam to get rid of it. He is good and kind and only wants to protect me. I am horrible for suspecting otherwise.

CHAPTER SEVEN

Eleven Weeks Before

I'm splashing around in the creek outside when Sam comes out, stretching and yawning. He's been napping so, so much lately. Sometimes it feels like he's always either gone or napping, and we haven't been having as much fun as we used to. Even his medicine doesn't seem to make him completely well anymore.

Abby, get back in here! It's not safe!

It is too safe! I yell back. *There's nobody here. Who can hurt me?*

You just shouldn't be out there, he says. *You don't even have any clothes on.* It's kind of true, kind of not. I have *some* clothes on. I'm in my underwear. It's chilly out but not cold enough to get me sick.

Sammy, don't be so silly. It's the people who are bad out there, not the nature. All of this is ours, anyway, I say, spinning around with my arms spread wide. The tickle of the cold water and the minnows swimming around my ankles make me laugh.

For once, Sammy doesn't have anything to say. He mutters something, but I can't hear him.

What? I shout.

Just be careful! he yells. This time I hear him, but I pretend not to anyway.

I can't hear you, I holler back. *Come closer!*

I wait until Sammy is close to the edge, then I dunk my arms in the water and splash as hard as I can. I come up laughing because his face is dotted with crystal water and his clothes are soaked. I expect him to laugh back, but his face looks irritated; I know because his mouth is shaped into a scowl. I sigh. He's been so moody lately. Nothing I do seems to make him laugh. I narrow my eyes and stare into his. What happened to my soul? The other half is drifting away.

Please, Sam, I say in my head.

I'm not sure, I feel him answer.

Have fun. Be easy, I think at him. It's easier to love than hate.

Not so, he thinks back at me. For some people, it's the other way around.

But not us, Sammy. Not you.

No, not us, he agrees silently.

And now he's shucking off his shoes and stripping off his jeans, and he's splashing out in the water toward me and scooping handfuls of it and tossing them on my cold, bare skin. My skin rises in goose bumps, and my heart rises in joy. We still have our special link. We are still woven of the same thread, even though he's been different.

We play for a while, and it feels so freeing and good to

be out here with him, as if our world has opened up with big possibilities. We play until the sky turns dusk and the sun can't ease our goose bumps any longer. When we go inside, he bundles me in a blanket and we make a fire. Sam's cheeks are rosy. He looks healthier than when he came home today.

You look good, Sam-Sam, I say. *You should play outside more.*

I would if I could, he says. *But I'm busy.*

Yeah, busy at Sid's, I mutter. *The mystery man.* Sam jerks back angrily.

That was rude, he says. I'm surprised. I meant nothing by it.

I was just joking around, Sam, I say. But he is silent. Lately, he jumps on me for everything. After a few more minutes, he's OK again, and he puts his arm back around me. We cuddle for a while. And I begin to be aware of his shirtless body against mine. My nerves begin to rise toward him the way they always do when we're close. It's been so long. I snuggle deeper and begin to kiss lightly at his neck. He wiggles away a little.

I don't understand, I say.

Nothing, Abby. I just don't feel like it right now.

You never feel like it anymore.

Stop exaggerating, he tells me. And so here we are in a stiff silence again. His arm is around me, but it feels like dead weight. I don't understand. He must not find me beautiful anymore. I'm not sure how or why that's possible. I wiggle out from under the blanket and under his arm and go to bed. I can't be close to him when he finds me so repulsive. It hurts too much.

Just as I am beginning to doze off, I feel him climb into bed with me. He kisses my cheek, my neck. I am afraid to turn in case he will stop. He kisses his way down my back, then back up, then turns my cheek to the side so I have to face him. He kisses me on the mouth, and all my hostility drifts away. I kiss him back and back for a long time, and I want more, but I can feel him slowly pulling away. He kisses me on the cheek a few more times and then settles back on the pillow, wrapping his arms around me tight. He falls asleep almost right away, but I am left the same as I was before. He has given me enough to ease my anger but not exactly what I want. I want him to want what I want. I see something beautiful in myself, but I must be repulsive and undesirable to him. The memory of his kisses fails to soothe me to sleep.

CHAPTER EIGHT

Ten-and-a-Half Weeks Before

Time passes so quickly.

I sit with Sammy on the roof of a tall building. It is night, and all the stars in the sky make a magic show just for us. I lay my head in his lap.

Tell me again how we met, I beg. We have known each other for a very long time, since long before he saved me from the fire. Sam says we have known and loved each other for longer than infinity, even though I can't remember it. Because of the way I feel about him, it must be true.

You were sitting on a cloud, he starts.

I thought it was a mountain?

No, Abby. He shakes his head. *A cloud. I remember because your toes were flecked with dew and your whole body was damp.*

Then what? I ask. He is running his fingers through my hair. He bends to kiss my temple. My heart beats staccato the way it always does when he's close.

Then the cloud started to break up, he continues. *Turn into mist or rain or something. And you began to fall.*

So . . . ?

Shhh, be patient! He pauses to think. *You fell and fell, for maybe a mile, and I saw you in the sky. You were a tiny speck that got bigger and bigger with each moment, and you were moving very fast. But luckily, I was sitting on a terrace, watching. And since I didn't have anything better to do . . .*

I laugh and bite his thigh playfully. Sammy loves to tease.

Anyway, he continues, *since I didn't have anything better to do, I thought, What the heck? I'll save this girl. So I climbed up the side of the building on the fire escape to the very top, like how we got here now. Except I had to do it fast, like six or eight times as fast as we got up here tonight. Because you were dropping like a rock, faster and faster. And just as I got to the top, you were above me, so I leaped off the building and grabbed you.*

But weren't you worried that you would fall, too? And we'd both wind up a pile on the ground?

Ah, mija, he purrs in my ear. *I never worry for my own safety when I have you to think of.*

And you were right not to worry, because we were fine, I finish. *The End.*

That isn't the end! We were only fine because I managed to catch a tree branch on the way down, then shimmy down the tree trunk with you on my back. Otherwise we would have gone splat on the pavement.

Right. And then I went home.

No, then you knelt down and kissed my feet and pledged

your life to me, since I had saved you. You didn't know me, but you vowed to love me forever.

Did not! I laugh. I wriggle with happiness.

You did, mija. *That is how it happened.*

I press my face into his stomach and wrap my arms around his back. He is right. The story is different each time. But sometime, somewhere in each version, I need him to save me, and when he does, I vow to love him forever. I hold on to the moment and enjoy him while I can, and for a while we are the way we were all those weeks ago when he scooped me up and brought me home.

CHAPTER NINE

Ten Weeks Before

Sam and I are having a picnic. I've convinced him it's
OK to be outdoors together if we stay close to our home.
He's moody again, irritable. I wonder if he is feeling
depressed. I am hurt that he might feel this way when he
has me to provide so much happiness. We are reclined
next to each other on the grass, interpreting cloud animals. Doing so gives me a vague, pleasant sensation of
familiarity. My stomach is round and full from the feast
we had: meats for him, cheeses for me, ice cream for us.

Sam, I say to him, *I love you more than I could possibly
love anyone. The feeling might not even be real, it's so big. It's
bigger than this world.*

Me, too, he says, rolling to face me.

No, I say. *You don't understand. I love you so much it's
painful to breathe.*

I know, mija, he says. *I do, too.*

*But I can't even picture anyone else. You are like a white
hole to me, because you can't be a black hole because of the
negative implication, but it all means the same thing. I'm not
even sure anyone else is alive in this world besides us.*

Sam laughs, but I can tell he is getting impatient with
me. He thinks all I do these days is talk about how I feel

and explore the notion of *us*, and he wants to do other things. To take long naps and read books and talk about them before taking more long naps. It bothers me that it doesn't match with what I want and need right now, because I feel we should be so attuned to each other that our desires shouldn't have to be spoken aloud.

Since he's drifted off, I take a walk by myself. What I'm feeling in this moment seems too important not to say. I wonder how to say it in a way he'll listen. I splash through the creek and up the dirt path and don't worry at all that I must be trailing mud prints into our home. I head for my sketch paper and write what is in my heart:

Sam. I have loved you since we met, and I love you still. Even before I ever saw you, I was waiting for you. You fascinate me. You are my love; I cannot feel for another what I feel for you. It stretches beyond anything earthly to something spiritual, and I could never run from it even if I were to try. I don't believe that what we have is knowable to anyone else. In these books we read, what others call love is ordinary. What we have is not of this world. Even if we spent a lifetime apart, these feelings would never fade. You are my heart, my soul. You are me. Nothing can ever change it. When we are apart, my mind is elsewhere, and my heart is reaching for yours across the space that separates us.

Abby

I fold it in half and place it on his pillow where he will see it right away when he comes in. I am satisfied. I walk outside again with one of Sam's books and cool my ankles in the creek. I walk down from Sam a ways, so I don't disturb him while he naps. I don't bother waking him up anymore; he's either too groggy or too grouchy when I do. I settle down with this book, *The Picture of Dorian Gray*. Sam has so many, and he really loves them, possibly more than me. He loves to talk with me about them. He says understanding the classics is the best way to understand the world as it really is. He opens my mind and teaches me how to think. None of these books, though, make me shudder like the *Inferno*, where people betray those close to them with no remorse. Even so, I keep coming back to it, reading its pages again and again until the ink is permanently smudged by the oils in my fingers and Sam's, too, I guess. It points me to the things I should be afraid of. It speaks of the world I need to avoid, a world full of hardened souls. I need it because of this. I like to keep the book close to me, and Sam doesn't seem to mind. When I read it, it seems like everything is crafted from black soot, everyone formed around a rotten core. *Dorian Gray* is like that, too, but not quite as awful as the other.

I sit and read until I begin to grow cold and I have a hard time seeing the words anymore. Then I wander back inside. Sam is awake now. He slipped back inside without me noticing and is sitting on ground with his back against the bed, reading his own book. My note is crumpled in a ball beside him. When I walk in, he looks up quickly.

Didn't you like it? I ask, settling down next to him on the floor.

No. I mean yes, I liked it. But isn't there anything else you think about, Abby?

Of course, I say.

Like what? His tone is rude and annoyed, and it hurts me. I don't know what I've done wrong.

I read your books. I think of what to do in the day.

Anything else?

Now I am getting mad. *Yes, Sam,* I say. *In fact, I do think of other things. I think back to a past I can't remember. I think about what is so wrong with me that I can't remember my own life. I think hard about why I feel pain instead of memories. I wonder all the time what has happened to me to make me like this. And I wonder why everything out there is evil, why I can't leave, why I feel this fear, what you're protecting me from.*

When I am finished, he is silent for a while.

I suppose it's easier to think of the things in your note, he says.

Yes. I nod.

He squeezes my forehead and kisses me on the shoulder. *Oh,* mija, he says. *You are such a little fawn. I'm sorry, baby. I'm sorry for getting upset.*

I bite my lip so I won't feel the tears that want to come. I nod again.

Ten Weeks Before

It is morning. I wake with a headache from thinking and worrying about Sam's reaction to my note. I woke up a few times in the night, and he was not in bed with me; the light was on, and he was busying himself with something on the couch. He is not in bed with me now, either. I feel as though I need hours more sleep, but when I try to close my eyes again, they pop open as if they're controlled by taut little wires in my lids. I roll on my other side, toward Sam's part of the bed. Where Sam should be, there is a stack of papers tied with a rope. I pick them up.

For the little fawn, they read. My heart quickens. I thumb through the pages, twelve in all. And I glance over to where he lies, asleep again on the couch. This is what kept him up all night.

Darling *mija,* it begins.

> *I cannot tell you how much you mean to me. But first,*
> *let me start with the basics, the things that drew me*
> *to you in the beginning. It was your skin at first, the*
> *soft sexiness of it. When I saw it, I knew it would feel*
> *the way it looked: like rich, thick milk. And later, after*
> *I had stopped being so fascinated by your skin that I*

was finally able to look at the rest of you, I was not disappointed. That nose of yours kept me intrigued for weeks. Its sweet, narrow little slope reminds me of Catullus's poems to Lesbia. It makes me want to be a poet, too, just for the fun of seducing you that way. I fell in love with the way you first looked at me with your beautiful, trusting eyes. Still filled with wonder, they never fail to thrill me. From the beginning, I have loved protecting you, taking care of you, keeping you secure. And your smile. When I was first able to get you to smile . . . it blew me away. Your smile is the most beautiful thing I have ever seen. Its tentative grace, its trusting curve. These things all put together add up to what you are: the epitome of femininity. All these qualities make me more of a man, make me stronger. You are the reason men from the beginning of time have found women to inspire them. Those women are their muses. You are my muse.

But beyond that, you are my life. I have found that no one interests me the way you do. Your brain works in so many ways; your thoughts are unfailingly sweet and innocent, but they are never trivial. You inspire me in a way no one else has. As long as I am alive, you will never have to be alone. I will never let that happen.

It continues on with words and phrases that mirror my own thoughts. It is the single most romantic thing

I may over possess. I sit with it for over an hour; that is how long it takes me to finish it. When he wakes up, he looks over at me from the sofa, and our eyes meet. He comes to sit at the foot of the bed, looking disheveled and penitent. He looks at me and I look at him, and then he tucks me into his arms, and as usual, we do not need to say anything. It would take ten languages, not just one, to say aloud what we tell each other in one instant with our hearts.

CHAPTER ELEVEN
Nine-and-a-Half Weeks Before

Ever since I read Sam's letter, the emotional things that once plagued me no longer do. I don't wonder if he feels how I do anymore, and I know I was wrong for being worried. But it doesn't change his moodiness, and he is still snapping at me from time to time. He seems dreamier, fatigued, and more eager to be left alone. And when he is awake, and we are together, the thing that frightens me is physical.

Sam no longer wants me the way I want him. I am forced to wonder as before if I am hideous or if part of me disgusts him. He kisses me and hugs me but never seeks me out in any other way. I am more confused than ever. Even now, as I lie next to him practically naked, or prance around the room in my underwear in the middle of the day, I don't provoke more than a glance. He is so quiet, so secretive. Then at night he is restless. He is sweaty all the time, and sometimes he gets sick. I want to know his secrets. I don't want to bother him, but I can feel the words bubbling out of me like a geyser. My willpower is not enough to stop them.

Sam? I say, tentatively. I watch as he looks up from his novel and grits his teeth, already annoyed.

I just want to know what's wrong, I say. *I know there's something.*

I don't know how many ways I can tell you that nothing *is wrong.*

I know, I know, I hastily tell him. *It's just that . . .*

What?

You never touch me anymore.

You're crazy. You're making up problems.

It's not true! You haven't touched me in ages.

Stop exaggerating, Abby. I'm just busy. He turns back to his book.

Busy what? I say, angry myself now. *Busy reading? Busy with your friend Sid?*

Stop it, he tells me through gritted teeth. *Stop talking right now.*

You can't say that to me! I shout. I'm feeling bold, so I press on. *Why are all of these other things in your life more important than me!*

He rustles his book and slaps it down on the nightstand.

Well, Abby, he says semisarcastically, *since you asked so nicely, I may as well tell you.*

I wait, feeling ashamed of my outburst before he's even begun to really talk.

You see, he says. *I am out of my medicine. Sid will not give me my medicine because I am out of money. But you never worry your pretty head about those things, do you? Money?*

What's that? You probably don't know. Or maybe you think you have stacks of it sitting in that drawer next to you.

I am shocked. We have never talked like this before.

What is wrong with you, Sam? I ask. *Why do you need medicine from Sid?*

We all have our secrets, Abby, he says. *I'd prefer if you don't ask me about mine.* His words pierce me deep. We have never worried about money. Sam goes out and he brings things home, and that is that. He's right that money has never crossed my mind. And now that I know why Sam's been strange, I feel guilty and sorry. But most of all, distant. He has pulled away from me and there is nothing I can do, because the harder I fight to draw him close again, the further he goes.

CHAPTER TWELVE

Nine-and-a-Half Weeks Before

Her hair is waist-long, and her body is a skinny vixen. She is sex.

Is she a whore? I ask him. *Where did you find her?* I have never felt this fury.

Be nice, Sam tells me as she glares.

Why should I? I am angry. He was gone for hours, and now he comes back with *this*, like she is a beautiful exotic puppy he wants to make into his pet. I glare back at her.

She's an old friend, Abby. She needs my help.

Didn't take you very long, she cuts in, eyeing me up and down.

I didn't know, Sam whispers short and quick, as if he doesn't want me to hear. *You told me you were gone for good.*

Turns out I'm not, she says. *Well, you never could fend for yourself out here, isn't that right?*

Sam looks at the ground. *I didn't plan for it,* he says. *But we're all here now.*

Thanks, anyway, she tells him, and she turns to go.

No! Sam grabs her wrist. *You'll sleep there.* He gestures toward the other bed, the one I slept on my first two nights, before I began to share his.

That one. Of course. She smiles again, like it's a sad little joke. Then she nods and heads for the bed, falling asleep almost as soon as her thin frame touches it.

Sam ignores me for several minutes. This isn't fair! I am confused and boiling over with angry panic. But I can't stand it when we're angry, so I whine.

How was I supposed to react, Sammy? This is our house!

This place is mine, he says through gritted teeth. *Not yours.*

I feel as if I have been punched. I want to throw up. How can he be so cruel? I curl onto our bed and cry bitterly. He storms back out of the cave.

Only now do I look at her starving frame. She is so frail, light enough to walk on water. She is beautiful, too. Her veins show through her skin. She's shaking, so I stand up and pull the blanket around her shoulders. As I tuck it around her, I notice the dozens of scars that crisscross her wrists. New, pink scars layered upon old. I am frozen in horror. Her eyes pop open and she stares at me, and I stare back.

Thank you, she whispers. Her eyes don't match her wasted body.

When Sam comes back, I cajole him back to bed with me. He plays angry for a while; then finally, I feel his arm around me, and my panic subsides.

But not entirely. How will it be, now that there are three?

CHAPTER THIRTEEN

Nine Weeks Before

Amanda pretends to be my friend, but I know she was sent here to ruin me. It has been days and days, so long I can't count, but at least a month if not some other indiscernible length of time. Yesterday I thought she was beautiful, but today I think she is Medusa. Her face wrinkles and her smile-grimace is ugly. Ugliness did not exist before she arrived. I can't help but resent her.

I am not certain Amanda is human. Some days I think she is a demon and this is a test. A test where she threatens to eat my soul and steal my love. I feel my soul deteriorating in her presence most of the time, then other times her sweet loveliness betrays me and restores my heart just enough that I can breathe, survive, and feel. And then it all happens again.

He brought me a birthday cake. Sam tells me it's my birthday and that I am seventeen today. I don't feel older. I don't feel any different at all. I suspect he is lying, try-ing to get me out of my mood. The cake is four tiers high and layered with coconut bits and covered in tiny sparkling candles. I went to blow them out, and they wouldn't blow out, and Amanda laughed and laughed, and I saw some of that ugliness she brought with her that never existed for me before. I didn't make a fuss; I just stood and walked over to the old writing desk, and here I sit now, writing and sketching. My pencil sketches the same face each day. It looks like Amanda, but if Amanda were younger and softer and had more light in her eyes. My pencil has drawn this face ever since it began to visit me in my dreams at night. Sam and the girl talk and laugh behind me. I wish I had gotten some cake before I decided to be stubborn. Amanda has pushed her chair in and walks toward me. She places her hand on my shoulder.

Happy Birthday, Abby-cakes, she whispers. My heart lifts just a little. She's brought me a piece. I hold it on my lap, where it balances precariously against my knees. Amanda sits on the ground with her own legs bent so she can rest her arms on them and her chin on her arms. About half the cake is gone before I notice her staring at me curiously.

You really like it, don't you? she says wonderingly. *You're not just pretending.*

What do you mean? I ask. *It's delicious!*

Then she leans toward me and whispers more quietly so Sam can't hear: *Abby, it's disgusting. It's hard as a rock and starting to mold—a dog probably wouldn't even eat it. Sam found it in the garbage bin behind the bakery downtown.*

I am so angry that I spit out my last bite, which has

indeed become hard and tasteless in my mouth. It's as if her words changed the cake to sawdust like magic. I was never this emotional before Amanda arrived. I don't know why she's always trying to spoil things. Sam must see we're not getting along, because he rushes to my side. The good thing about Amanda being here is that Sam has been more like his old self. Protective of me, caring.

What did she say to you? he asks me, glaring at Amanda at the same time. I shake my head in response, and Amanda smiles wickedly. I refuse to play Amanda's games, although it occurs to me briefly that if he thinks she's being cruel, it's maybe a way for me to get all of Sam back for myself. But I can't look like a baby, and Amanda makes me so nervous that I'm sure if I play it wrong, I'll color his reaction the wrong shade. He glares at Amanda again, and she just shrugs.

I can't help but notice that her mean look is gone and there's sadness in her eyes. She is staring at the cake as if it is something to be afraid of. I focus on her thinness, and the way her ribs protrude from her chest more prominently than her breasts. Then it occurs to me that the reason Amanda wants me to think the cake is old and moldy is probably because she *needs* to think the cake is old and moldy, so she won't want to eat it. People like that, girls who give food so much power, need it more than the rest of us. They lust after it like some of us lust after the body. But they fear it, too, because it holds more power over them than they know how to handle. Food becomes a golden serpent instead of just nourishment.

I feel sorry for her. I know all about it because I knew someone else like that, once, someone who always had hunger in her eyes. I try to think who, but I can't quite remember. I can't think of anything past my headache. I think maybe I could reach it sometime, way in the back of my head, but not today. Not while it hurts like this. I look at Amanda and shudder because the eerie déjà vu of it all has crept its way under my skin. Sometimes I'm sympathetic to Amanda even though my brain cries out not to be. After all, she is taking Sam away from me. But something about her is so familiar that I have all these natural warm feelings for her. I meditate on this while my head pain slides away. I focus on what's in front of me until the ache is gone altogether. It helps, doing that.

It's OK, I say quietly to her when Sam has gone, busying himself at the sink. I know why you can't enjoy it. I savor the rest of my cake, letting my eyes slide over her sharp elbows and thin wrists one more time, then back to her face, where she is shaking her head as if to say, *You don't know anything at all.* I stand up and walk away with my plate. This girl turns everything topsy-turvy. My stomach is sick from it.

CHAPTER FOURTEEN

Eight-and-a-Half Weeks Before

Amanda bends over me, so close I can smell her.

I love her I hate her I want her I want to be her.

We are making dinner together.

Go over to the fridge, I say, *and grab me a salmon fillet.* She's too close. I don't understand my complicated feelings toward her. Amanda reminds me of someone good and something bad. She makes me nostalgic for someone I can't remember. It's a feeling of happy pain. Sometimes I crave it, and sometimes it makes me glad I've forgotten.

Fridge! She howls with laughter. *Salmon! You're too funny, Abby.* She ruffles my hair condescendingly and prances away as I glower. She's always teasing me, mocking me slightly, not enough to be malicious but just enough to sound imperious. I see Sam shoot her a warning look—he knows how she bothers me. I don't like feeling like the outsider. But I lighten up as Amanda forgets the food, instead grabbing my arms and whirling me around the room with her as she sings. Amanda has the most beautiful voice; it fills the room, and it's enough for me to understand what Sam sees in her.

Later, we are getting ready for bed when she gives me a funny card she made. It's in the shape of a pig, folded like origami, and it has a poem inside along with a thin, woven bracelet.

A friendship bracelet, she says, smiling. *Let me tie it on you. You ever been to California, Abby?* she asks absently as she's tying. *It's beautiful there, and always warm. That's where I'm gonna go someday, when I save up the cash. California. It's paradise on earth.*

She seems almost like she's talking to herself, but I nod anyway, letting myself wallow in her attention. She frowns over the bracelet; it's far too big for my wrist, and she doesn't want to cut it, so we drape it around my ankle instead. I step back and hold my foot out to admire the purple and orange and gold threads against my skin. Amanda is wonderful. Her beauty fills my heart.

But she isn't always like this. Sometimes she screams and flies into rages, throwing things at Sam. She never throws things at me, but she is not above giving me cold stares and ignoring me when I speak to her. Other times, she cries all night.

Sam doesn't see her as troubled, only moody and passionate.

It's what I love most about her, he tells me often. *It's why I brought her home in the first place. She's color to your gray.*

I think it's a cruel thing to say, but when I sulk, he says he doesn't mean it that way, only that he thinks we're both perfect and beautiful, and when I ask him if he thinks she is more beautiful, he only says that I shouldn't worry because Amanda's like a sister to him, since they have a lot in common. Then why do they go out together late at night, when they suppose I am asleep? Why has Amanda started taking Sam to Sid's, instead of me? He never elaborates what exactly it is that ties them together that leaves me out. He must know, though, what it does to me, his leaving me for her.

CHAPTER FIFTEEN
Eight Weeks Before

The room is black magic around us. I feel his fingers prod my back gently, and when I turn, his neck is ready and welcome. I have craved this for weeks as if it could heal my soul of the horrible jealousy that nests inside me. I burrow into him. All of Sam's angles fit into my curves; we are clay figures bent and posturing. I purr as he rubs his body on mine. Then we're grabbing at each other all over and frantic as if we want to use our inadequate hands to touch whole bodies, every part at once. I grab a handful of his back. His skin is smooth and soft in my fingers. His flat, hard stomach muscles strain against my curvier ones. I try to push my body through his skin to meet his insides. I want to live inside of his skin, wrap him around me like a blanket.

We hunt and grab and hold and dig. I feel his tongue on my collarbone, my shoulder, then my breasts, my stomach, moving lower still. We are needy, desperate. Our sweat mixes, our shallow breathing combines. I rise toward him, keeping rhythm, pressing my hips into his. And when we are closer than ever before, as close as I think we can be and still be alive and separate, I look up into his eyes.

His eyes are filled with something that isn't me. He stares past me. I don't know where he is. When I see his face, I am stricken. It breaks our body magic. He notices and looks down.

What's wrong?

You aren't looking at me. You're looking at someone else.

No, baby. There's no one else.

He comes back down from over me and holds me, but it is too late. The magic is gone. He says all the right things in my ear, but I don't believe any of them. Lies, all lies. I don't believe a word he says, but I play a wicked game with myself anyway and pretend to trust him. Sometimes I wish I had someone here to tell me what to do. Someone other than Sam or Amanda, I mean.

He is sad.

I don't want us to be separated.

Never, we will never be separated, I reassure him, even though I don't know anything for sure. I curl into myself. If we move an inch, everything that has happened just now will disappear. We are hanging on to each other by a slim, weak tendril, not the spiderweb kind that can hold anything but the spun-glass kind that snaps. Sammy calls this love, but it's uglier than that.

CHAPTER SIXTEEN

Eight Weeks Before

My eyes dart around for Sam. She's holding the picture close to my face, so close it fills my field of vision. I can't do this today. I can't handle her alone. I feel so anxious.

He's not here, she says. *He's gone again. How does that feel, Abby?*

I blink back tears. He left me here with her. Is that what she is to me? A babysitter, so he can get me off his hands?

Focus! She shouts it at me violently. Her eyes are wild, and her hair is a tangled mess, black and furious. She looks paler and sicker than before, and bruises race up her arms. Yet she is still a vision of beauty. Next to her, I am ordinary. It is no wonder he rarely wants me.

Now, she says again, more quietly, *what do you see? It's a Rorschach, Abby. We want to understand you.*

Amanda might very well be crazy. She's a dancing skeleton. Maybe the *we* means her and her bones. She made a test for me to take, using my paper and a bunch of ink. She broke a pen in half and spilled the ink all over the paper. Now she's holding it in front of my head like a trophy.

Tell me!

I focus hard. If I say the wrong thing, she may well attack me. She has never done it, but I expect it. I am feeling skittish. This is all wrong. I woke up this morning, and everything was a different color. Amanda looked ghoulish, and when that happens, which has been only once before, I know that something is very wrong inside my head. Everything feels just one degree off, as though I am still walking in my dream. And what happened in the dream? I can't place it, but I woke up with a sinking in my heart that has left me jittery all day, and Amanda is only making it worse. It is as if she stepped right out of the strange, skewed dream right onto the fabric of real life. Like she can hop from one place to another. I wonder if she can. It would be remarkable. I wonder if she can control it the way one would control a time machine or if it is something that happens at random, which would account for her crazy mood swings. I stop wondering and start focusing because it's obvious she's impatient.

It's a porcupine, I say. It looks mostly like a big round blotch of nothing, to me, but there are enough long, sharp lines to make *porcupine* a passable answer. And I think it will probably please her to some extent.

Aha! she shouts. *Porcupine! I knew you were one fucked-up kid, Abby, but I didn't know it was* this *bad.*

I am on the edge of my seat. Something about her voice screams malice. This isn't a silly game to her. She looks deranged. I am especially uneasy because I don't know where this is going. Amanda dances around the room, still holding the picture.

Porcupines are warriors, Abby. They'd never stay inside this hole like you do, hiding away all day, shriveling up into nothingness like you!

I am quiet.

They're sharp on the outside, warm on the inside. Is that what you see when you look at yourself, Abby? Is that who you think you are?

I don't know what to say, so I nod. She's gesturing violently and erratically. She looks like a puppet whose strings are being pulled by several different hands all at once. *Wrong!* she shouts, pointing one finger at me. *You're just a weak, spineless kid! You've got no thorny parts. You're no warrior. You're a victim.* She hisses the last word, then she steps closer, leaning her head so close to mine that our lips almost touch. *You let people use you, Abby. You let Sam use you.*

No, I whisper.

Yes, she sneers. *You think Sam's yours, but I've known him my whole life. Sam and I are the same, Abby. I know him better than anyone, and I know he's using you just because he can.*

I stand up. I don't know where I'm going to go, but I've got to get out of here. The world is tilting sideways, and I can't keep upright. Nothing is clear. But I feel her hand on my wrist. That's enough.

Let me show you, she says. *You can be like me. You can make things happen. Sam doesn't love you, but it doesn't need to matter.*

At these words, something inside me shuts off. She can't think he loves her instead of me. She can't. I look over at her and it's worse than bad; it's like a horror film I can't turn away from. She has the thin blade of a razor against her arm and she's cutting herself, and blood is streaming out. Then she looks up at me, and her face is twisted and awful, but it's not her face anymore; it's the face of the girl from my dreams. And I look back down at her wrist, and blood isn't pouring out at all; it's sparkling red rubies that cascade from her arm to the floor. I scream and scream, and my head cries out for mercy, and witch-dream-girl smiles wider. I don't know what's happening. I don't know what I'm seeing anymore. Then Sam's arms are around me.

What are you doing to her! he shouts at witch-dream-girl, who has turned back into Amanda.

Nada, she says back, stepping around me to place one palm on Sam's cheek. She's beautiful again for him. Vile for me, lovely for him. Sam grabs her palm and turns it so her wrist is facing him.

Fuck, Amanda, he says.

It's nothing, Sam-Sam, Amanda tells him. *Just a scratch. See?* She licks her wrist once, twirling her tongue around until it's covered with her own blood, and only a tiny bit remains, seeping slowly through the cut.

That's not enough, Amanda, says Sam. *What the hell happened here?*

She shrugs as if she's exhausted. *Oh, lighten up, Sam. We both know you're no longer the golden boy; you gave that life up a long time ago, so do me a favor and don't act like someone's dad, 'K? Anyway, I was just having a little fun. You know I'm not a cutter anymore. Who knows what* she *thinks happened? We both know she's loony tunes.* She presses her wrist against her shirt and when she pulls it away, it's a new inkblot: a constellation of tiny red droplets. It had looked like so much more before, a tsunami of blood. Then she turns to me, where I am shaking against Sam's shoulder. *I'm really sorry, Abby,* she says, then kisses me on the cheek. She might even be sincere. But I'm not sure it matters. I am more afraid of what I saw than of her. If I could only understand what I saw, I would have nothing to be afraid of.

All right, then, says Sam, patting me one last time on the shoulder. *Amanda, I need you for a few minutes.* I am reeling. Is it as simple as that? *We'll be right back,* mija, he says to me. Then they walk out together, and I watch her hand slide from his shoulder and trail down to his lower back, where it rests because he does not move it away. She looks back at me and winks, and then they're gone and I'm alone, needing him, feeling adrift without him in this universe he created.

CHAPTER SEVENTEEN
Eight Weeks Before

Dream Girl is back. Her hair is normally tar-colored, but this time it's coated in a red halo. I reach out to touch it; it is flickering orange, yellow, red, and it's so lovely, she looks lit up like an angel. But when my finger touches her halo-crown, my skin bubbles as if it's on fire. I feel no pain, but I draw it back anyway. My finger is black and blistered.

Dream Girl laughs and laughs.

Don't you know me, Abby?

Amanda? *I say.* Are you Amanda?

Not Amanda, Abby.

I want to know. Please tell me!

I can't believe you'd forget me so easily.

But I've forgotten everything, *I tell her.* There's not one thing I know.

You know more than you think.

I wake just a little, feel myself pulling out of the nightmare as my head pulses angrily. But there is something important there, something I need. I will myself back to sleep.

She glares at me, then begins to wail, clutching at her hair as the flames spread. Fire is coming from every orifice: there are flames from her ears and smoke from her nose and she is breathing balls of it. She pulls tufts of hair from her skull and watches them burn up in her palms. But she does not touch me. She never goes after me.

I am frozen in horror, but mostly unafraid. As I watch her die, I feel the part of my soul that loves her leaving the rest of me behind. I love her so much, and she's leaving me.

When she's reduced to ash, I grab it in handfuls and stuff it into my mouth, swallowing her down in an effort to keep her close. Only her eyebrow ring is not swallowable; I can't ingest that. It sticks in my throat, and I cough it back up. I use it to puncture my own eyebrow. She is consuming me. But that part of my soul is still gone.

I wake up from my dream crying and alone. It's the same dream I've had before; the same girl has been haunting me, and I only wish I knew why she's chosen me. I look around the room for Sammy, but he's out; Amanda is gone, too. I don't know what they're doing and why they always wait until I'm asleep to do it, but it almost doesn't matter. Usually when Sammy's gone like this, he brings me back sweets, the caramel-filled kind that he likes better than I do, just in case I've noticed his absence. He wants to seal in the hole he left with sticky caramel. But I don't care about that. I only want him here to comfort me when I wake up like this. Before Amanda came, he never would have left me alone for this long.

I lie awake for minutes, maybe hours, until the passage

of time is indiscernible. Finally I hear their voices. Amanda sounds happy, drunk.

Carry me in, Sammy, she says. *Over the threshold.*

Whatever you say, little one.

I hear her material on his material as she climbs up his back, and I barely see her legs latch around his waist, but what I don't see I make up for using my imagination. I picture her face pressed into his neck and her chest against his back and her hair drifting down his shoulder and his heart pulsing faster at the contact. I tremble. My whole body convulses angrily, afraid.

I watch their shadow become one, and they stumble farther into the room until Sam loses his balance and they tumble to the ground in a wriggling heap. Finally she kisses his cheek good night, and I can barely see her whispering something that I can't hear into his ear. I can picture his look of regret as she walks to her bed and he walks to mine. I can't say "ours" anymore because now he's given himself a choice, and he doesn't belong just to me. But without him, who am I?

He crawls into bed with me and wraps his arms around my ribs, but I know he's doing it because he can sense from my breathing patterns that I am awake and angry. And he's right. He should not have been out doing whatever he was doing with her. He should have been here when I woke up from my dream. He doesn't even try to apologize this time. My whole body recoils from his, and his arms have begun to feel more and more like a vise. I don't trust their sincerity; I think he must imagine they are clasping Amanda tightly, not me. If he'd been here, Dream Girl may not have come to terrify me, so no matter how hard he tries to fool me, I can't pretend to forgive him.

CHAPTER EIGHTEEN
I remember my mother.

Today I remembered something important. Once, long ago, I had a mother. I was sitting outside reading when I remembered it. It may have been the feel of the pages under my fingers or the glossy plastic cover on the book, the kind of cover that looks like it belongs in a library. Then it came to me in a sickening, panicked flash. I only saw it for an instant, and even as my head fought against its surge of dull pain, I fought to hold on to it. The entire memory may have lasted one second, or maybe two. It was more like an experience than anything else. With it came the rush of feelings, good and bad. I half want to forget it; thinking of it makes my stomach clench. But it is mine, one of the few things that are mine alone, and it's a treasure.

She is reading to me; it's my favorite book, selected from the same spot in the same library shelf each week. I have heard it a dozen times, but I love it. She pulls me onto her lap, and I lean back into the crook of her arm and the curve of her stomach and chest. Her big wool sweater tickles my cheek. I am small, three or four.

It's a fairy tale about a boy and a girl who love each other but are separated by an evil witch who wants the boy to marry her ugly daughter. The evil witch puts a spell on the girl, so the girl dies. The girl comes back as a ghost and watches as the ugly daughter impersonates her in an attempt to woo the prince. In the end, the evil witch and her daughter die in a horrible fire, and the girl comes back to life to be with her prince. I love the ending; it is my favorite part. As the woman reads, she conveys a message of love. I am hers and she is mine.

The memory is brief but important because it's a gift from my past. It left me shaking and nauseated, though intact. I never knew for sure whether I'd ever had a mother, and now I know that I had a good one who loved me. All of me is cold and hot and calm and provoked by this knowledge. It makes the pain easier to bear. I tuck it away because I can't think of it, really think of what it means, just yet.

CHAPTER NINETEEN
Seven Weeks Before

I'm watching them through the skylight. I'm standing on the chair, and I've pulled myself up to see and hear better. I have never seen them fight like this. I am thrilled; if they fight badly enough, he'll be all mine again. I've hated sharing him. She's clutching something in her hand. It looks like an old newspaper. It's tattered with wear. She's waving it at him, and now he's approaching her and trying to touch her arm, but she brushes his off. He tries to grab the piece of paper she's holding, but she grips it tight and it rips in half. Now they each have half of it. I wish I could know what it is, but I can't hear much of anything at all. Just some muted shouting and the sounds of anger. And maybe, possibly . . . my name?

I move closer to the skylight, poking my head partially outside and straining to hear. They don't notice me; they're too involved in their own furious words. Now I am able to catch some of them here and there.

. . . *is why,* says Amanda.

No, Sam says back. *No, give it to me.* He snatches at the scrap she still holds in her hand. I see printed words, a picture, what looks like half a headline in big bold letters, but I can't make out any of it.

It's her, isn't it? Her voice is louder than before, accusing. She jabs at the newspaper with one finger. Then Sam whispers something, and they turn their backs to me and their words fade, become muffled. They move away a few steps, still facing the other direction. I hear nothing now, but I can still see their figures set in battle stance.

Good. I hope they are fighting over me. I hope she's making him choose. Because I know deep down that if he has to, he will choose me over her. It is interesting watching Amanda become angrier. Even when she's been moody in the past, it seems a little too dramatic, as though she's putting on a show that doesn't quite reflect what she's really feeling. But this time, I see bits of her personality that I never quite noticed. Her face is set in a firm line, and her cheeks are flushed. She looks healthy in her anger. She looks as if she cares deeply about what she's saying. For an instant I wonder if she truly loves Sam as I do. I had not thought it was possible before. I thought for her it was something different. The desire to win, to have. Now she is stomping away from him, and he is shaking his head, looking furious. I wonder about his reaction, because don't these kinds of quarrels look different? Shouldn't one person look penitent, or desperate to ease the other? But what do I know of it? I hear Amanda stomping closer, so I jump off the chair and hastily push it back to its spot by Sam's desk.

I leap onto the bed and grab my sketch pad and pretend

as though I've been sketching this whole time. They both storm in a few seconds later. Sam looks as though he's swallowed something nasty, and Amanda looks a mixture of angry and frightened and confused. I wish I knew what happened. Amanda lies on her bed and turns her back to us. Sam comes over to me, and I am immediately glad. He is finally choosing me over her. Finally coming back to me, where he belongs. I sense that this is the end of Sam and Amanda, and my heart is leaping around inside in the utmost ecstasy. He sits at the foot of the bed, starting at my toes and kissing his way up the rest of me until his body is aligned with mine.

But something is wrong. I look at Amanda's back and see that it is shaking with sobs. My delightful feeling is muted by her pain.

What happened? I say to Sam.

Don't worry, mija, he whispers, but I can tell he's shaken up. *It's just Amanda being Amanda. It'll be fine.* Then what is that note of fear in his voice?

Sammy, I say, *please tell me if something is wrong.*

Nothing's wrong, mija.

Now he looks as if he is thinking hard. He pauses, then whispers hesitantly into my ear, low so Amanda can't hear: *I want you to come out with me tomorrow, Abby. I want you to meet Sid.*

You want me to meet your friend? I ask.

Yes, baby.

When, Sam? When do we go? I am so delighted, I am practically jumping out of my skin. This must mean that Sam *has* made a decision. He has chosen me. He is bringing me closer to him, letting me be a part of his life.

Shhh, baby. He motions his head toward Amanda. He must not want to hurt her feelings. Suddenly, I have no regard for Amanda at all. It's clear why she's crying; it's because I have won. She is no longer close to Sam's heart. My own heart is so warm and full of Sam; it is the happiest I've been in so long. I am so happy that his creased brow doesn't bother me at all. His worry for Amanda, because that is what it must be, can't affect me anymore. *Seven at night,* he says. *We'll go at seven.* I fall asleep after several hours of tossing and turning, like a child. And for once, my sleep is dreamless.

CHAPTER TWENTY

Seven Weeks Before

We're going to Sid's so I can meet him for the first time, and also for Sam's medicine. Sam asked me to dress up, to look pretty, and I am so excited for this and all it means for us that I am eager to please him. I want to look extra beautiful tonight. Being here with Sam is a cause to celebrate. Sam put on his nicer jeans, too — the ones without the holes, and the button-down shirt the man at the deli gave him as a present last month. He looks handsome, although a little nervous. I wonder if he's worried about whether Sid will approve of me. I am wearing a pink-and-white striped sundress that Sam brought me this morning. I don't know how he bought it; it still has the tags on it. It fits me perfectly, except in the chest. I think for my age I should have a bigger chest than I do, and it is my only big regret physically. It cinches my little waist nicely. It looks like a southern-belle dress because the skirt is so wide; if I tied a Hula-Hoop in it, I'd be a true Scarlett O'Hara. Amanda has been staring at Sam angrily all evening.

Beautiful, Sam says to me as we are leaving, deliberately ignoring her. It has been a long time since he has given me a compliment, and I can't help but be smug at the way he's treating the she-witch. I can tell he is a little anxious. He's clutching my hand tight, and it's sweaty. I've never seen him like this. I know he is hoping for his medicine.

When we arrive at Sid's, we sit on the sofa, sipping on the drinks Sid gives us in red plastic cups. We do this for a while, and the boys make uneasy small talk. Sid's just a normal guy, not much older than Sam or me. He's wearing jeans and sneakers and a white T-shirt. He doesn't look like anyone special. His house is plain inside. There's nothing here but a sofa and a coffee table and a few empty Chinese takeout containers and a guitar propped in one corner and a cat slinking around on the windowsill.

It's strange that they are so awkward together, Sam and Sid, even though they're friends. The drinks are strange, too. I thought they were glasses of mango juice at first, but now I notice some bitter taste behind the sweet. I sip until the world is hazy. I am not sure what world we are in right now. It seems like one or the other won't stick. I lean into Sam's shoulder and close my eyes, waiting for the world to settle. I allow my mind to drift, leaning farther into the soft leather couch cushions, as I wait for Sam and Sid to finish talking business. To finish talking about Sam's health, so Sid and I can get to know each other. Sid does not seem like the doctors I remember from Before. I have vague memories that might have happened to me or might have been something I saw on TV, but I remember doctors in sterile offices with white jackets and stethoscopes, a kind woman who whisked me to such places the second I got a sore throat. But everything is different with Sam, and I have gotten accustomed to it. So even though it is different tonight, I am not worried. We have been out together before. But the world has not spun like this any other time.

Their words are underwater. I don't hear anything anymore.

Sam is sitting next to me. His arm was around my shoulders, but now his hand is creeping up my thigh. It reaches higher, touching me tentatively, as if it is afraid. Then he is touching me where he touches only when we are both in our world, happy together and alone. It feels good then, but it is strange and foreign now. I feel another hand on me, this time on my chest. I struggle to open my eyes. I pry them open just slightly, and I see Sid next to me. I am being rude by falling asleep the first time we meet. But is it Sid's hand on my chest, under my dress? His other on my stomach, rubbing low? I try to move, but it is as if my mind is not connected to my body anymore, as if I am not a part of any world at all and my motor functions have ceased to operate. It isn't a bad feeling. I stop worrying and let go, float along the haze where I can feel nothing.

* * *

When I wake up later, I am curled up on the sofa as if nothing has happened. Sid is nowhere in sight. Sam is nudging me. He looks happy. There is a shine to his eyes that was missing before.

Did you get it, Sam? I ask sleepily.

Yes, baby, he says. Even though his eyes shine, something in them doesn't look right. He carries me home in his arms. I am small, but he hasn't been strong enough to carry me in a long time. I'm happy that he's gotten stronger. He puts me to bed carefully, because I am still too sleepy and sluggish to do it myself. He is being especially tender tonight. He touches my hair and whispers, "I'm sorry," over and over. I know somewhere deep down what he is sorry for, but just now I can't place it. I only need to sleep. He touches my hair for a very long time, until I drift away again.

CHAPTER TWENTY-ONE

Six-and-a-Half Weeks Before

Amanda's going out. She's slipping on a pair of shoes. They're lovely; their fabric is a rich and creamy leather. They're woven with a pretty space for her polished toes to poke through.

Peep-toe, she says.

Then something changes. Something wriggles in the back of my mind, and I rush after it and fight with it, wrestling. I halfway want it and halfway want to get rid of it. It's a memory. I am anxious and sweaty and teeming. It breaks its way in.

I am in a large store.

The shoes are all around me, but not the ones I want to find. I look down for them, because it is too far to look up for faces. That's how small I am. There are greeting cards on the shelves next to me. They're at eye level. Women's thighs are also at eye level, but not the thigh I am looking for. I can tell by the shoes.

I have gotten lost. Usually I wrap my arms around her cool, smooth knee, press my cheek right there against her, and don't let go. But somehow I have let go, and I am lost, wandering around this store, looking for my mother. I can't think what her shoes look like, but I will recognize them when I see them.

I walk up and down the aisles, my head pointed toward the floor. Black high heels with little gold buckles, flashy against this worn, patterned carpet. Brown loafers. Sneakers. None of them my mother. Then I see it: two feet in flat, tan, woven shoes, with a hole in the front for the toe to poke through. I lunge at this pair of shoes and grab the leg attached to them. I am safe. I am home.

Oh, hello, *a voice says. It is kind but unfamiliar. Only then do I look up. To my horror, I see a stranger's face peering down at me. It is not her at all; the shoes deceived me! I burst into tears, and the world is black. I back away from this unfamiliar woman.*

And then there is a pair of arms around me, and I am scooped up onto her chest where I am able to bury my face in her shoulders and neck. She found me. I looked for her, and I couldn't find her, but she came to me.

It's OK, *says the little girl who's standing next to her, a little older than me. She looks up at us sweetly.* Don't cry. Mommy's got you now, see? *I nod down at her, and then there is the lovely feeling that no matter what, she will always come to me. I will always be found, never alone.*

The memory fades.

But later, even long after the pain in my head is gone, an overwhelming and unexplained guilt remains.

CHAPTER TWENTY-TWO
Six Weeks Before

It's disgusting what you did, Sam. Amanda's voice reverberates into the room from outside where she sits. I can tell from her tone that she's upset. That's nothing new, though, so I don't pay much attention. Amanda's always upset, even when she's not upset. She exudes tense energy that makes her look constantly ill at ease. And she's especially frustrated all the time with me, because I am what she calls a *lethargic lump.*

And what exactly is that, Amanda? What is it that I did? Sam's tone warns her, but I know she isn't done. They're on the verge of another fight. I feel even more anger in the air than I did the last time they fought. I sketch harder in my journal, and the small girl peers up at me from one unfinished eye. The scene from my memory has been haunting me for days. It can only mean one thing: I had a family once. I let the knowledge roll around inside me where it makes me feel full and sickly empty all at once. I wonder and wonder how I got from who I was to who I am, from full to empty, connected to lonely; until the wonder is too much and I give up altogether, focusing on my drawing instead. It is an incomprehensible world in which we live.

Are you kidding? And it's not even just that. It's what you do every day. I can't believe I never noticed it before, how sick it is. You use her, you bait her, you encourage her fantasies. It's . . . She trails off. Then, more calmly, *It's sick, Sammy. Everything's so fucked up here.*

Abby's a thinking being. She can do whatever the hell she wants.

But she doesn't. She does whatever you want. She may as well be your pet, Sam. She's terrified of—

The rest of Amanda's sentence is muffled by a sob.

You used me, too, Sam.

I never asked you to do anything you hadn't done already.

My hand sketches the heart-shaped face and long, curled lashes of the woman. My back hurts where it is pressed up against the stone wall. There's a long pause.

Then, *She loves me,* he whispers to her. *I don't force her to be here.*

She doesn't know what love is. And you don't treat her like you love her.

I press the pencil hard on the paper, and it cracks. But not before it draws one tiny jewel in each ear. A mouth bow-shaped and meant for talking to me. Arms strong and meant for hugging me. Amanda's voice is getting shrill outside.

I can't take it, Sammy! I'm leaving. And if you want me to keep my mouth shut, you'll let me take her with me.

Shut up, Amanda.

You're not going to stop me, Sam.

He laughs scornfully. *What are you going to do, huh?*
You going to be a hero? Save your precious little Abby from
big bad Sam? You're a junkie; *Amanda, and how about the*
truckers in the big city? Were you too skinny? Too drugged
up? Business not booming like you thought? What was
it, anyway? Why'd the big plan fail, A.? Why'd you bother
crawling back here? I'd love to see what you plan to do for
Abby, run a tag-team operation? Make her just like you, so
you can feel better about yourself? You going to be the hero
here? You go right ahead.

I'm going to tell her, Sam. I can't keep it in any longer. I'm
going to tell her what you did. I'm going to take her away
from you. I'll take her out West with me to California. It's
warm there. We'll have a life. We'll get away from you.

I never asked you to come back! he shouts. *We were fin-*
ished! I was done with you; I found her, everything was fine.
She needs *me. You're meddling—that's all. You're just fuck-*
ing it all up. You came back and thought you'd mess with my
head and things would be like always, and it's driving you
crazy that I don't need you anymore.

I hear an angry howl and a tussle. I really don't like that
they are fighting. My hand goes right on drawing. Then
there are loud noises and the sound of cries, and now
Sam and Amanda are in the room. She grabs my wrist.

Wait, Amanda. I'm drawing. See? I show her my picture.

Isn't it nice, honey, she says. *Now, come on with me.* Then she's pulling me up off my feet, and I can only think that she's incredibly strong for someone so skinny.

Amanda, stop, I say. *Isn't this one better than the others?*

Yes. She grits her teeth hard. *Now, put it down. You're coming with me right now.* She rips my tablet from my hands and the paper tears, dividing the face in half. It lands on the floor at our feet. I scream long and loud. She's ripped my mother's face in half. I scream and scream and then Sam is between us.

Leave her alone, he says over my shrieking. He tries to pull Amanda away but she's too strong even for him. I'm afraid of her now, afraid she'll take me away from him.

Sammy, help, I say.

Don't look at him, Abby! Look at me! she shouts. Something inside me is waking up. Something about this isn't right. I stand still and let them fight over my parts. Maybe they'll divide me in two like the picture, and they won't have anything to argue about anymore.

Get OFF her! He screams this in her face and then slaps her, and she flies back and sobs on the ground, and I sob standing up. Then she's running, running away from this hell, and he's chasing her outside through the trees and instead of thinking of anything, I pick up my tablet and carefully line up the paper where it's ripped and finish my drawing, and when I'm done, I hang it up on the wall next to the others. There is a striking simi-larity. My mother in this picture looks like Dream Girl. Amanda is not that girl.

The room around me looks brighter in the last evening light and from outside, the sunset has washed away all traces of the ugliness that just happened here. It makes the stone walls glitter like a thousand tiny prisms, and I am blinded by the beauty of it all. The breeze carries in the scent of freesia, and as I soak up these very nice things, I am happy again and unworried.

CHAPTER TWENTY-THREE

Again I remember childhood.

I am five or six. I am opening a gift; it is my birthday. I tear off the wrapping and toss it aside.

Say cheese, *says a woman. Another woman who looks like her, but older and wrinkled, stands behind her. She wears a fudge-smeared apron. She waggles her tongue at me and flops her fingers behind her ears, making a silly face.*

I smile at them both.

The flash of a camera.

I pull out the ice skates. They're white with pink laces, for a figure skater. I can't wait until after I open the rest of my gifts. (There is a large stack of them on the wooden table where I sit.) I slip on the skates right away. I teeter to the door, and the older woman shakes her head at the scratches my blades leave on the floor.

I slide down the narrow pond-bank on my rear. The snow is cold through my jeans. I didn't stop to put a snowsuit on. Then I am on the ice; I am skating, faster and faster, and the wind is hitting my cheeks in sharp painful gusts. I laugh; I am freer than ever before. I slip and I fall; I get up and do it again. I try turns and jumps. I am becoming bolder. I can't get enough of this feeling.

I slip and fall again. This time, the blade of my skate

catches in a rut when I go down, and my ankle is twisted. I feel strong arms lift me up. They carry me back up the bank to the house, where I am deposited on a sofa in front of a fireplace. The younger woman wraps my ankle with thick gauze, brings me hot tea with milk and sugar. I am allowed to open the rest of my presents: a carousel music box, a silver charm bracelet. I love coming here; this place is peaceful, happy.

I want it, this memory and all the rest, despite the way it hurts.

CHAPTER TWENTY-FOUR
Six Weeks Before

It was an accident, he tells me when I ask where Amanda has gone. She was upset. He couldn't control her. He tried. He says I was there. That I held her hands behind her back, and he pushed her to the ground. He says I was jealous. That I watched him press his body weight against hers. He says he was trying to make her be quiet so he could comfort her, but holding her down didn't work. Amanda ~~has always been~~ was always strong and feisty. It ~~is~~ was a joke among us that I am the porcelain baby, she the snorting bull, Sam the circus master. I don't remember who came up with that joke. I don't remember any of this happening.

They got into a fight. Amanda ~~has been~~ had been edgy lately. Things were tense between Sam and me, Sam and Amanda, me and Amanda. Three's a crowd. She told me she wanted to leave. She wanted me to come. But it's not my fault I couldn't. She ~~knows~~ knew I can never leave Sam. I can't ever leave Sam. He knows my mind like it is his. And then she was gone into the fog. I don't know what happened after that.

He says he shouted her name. That he ran outside after her, and I stood just outside and watched them running, and for once, he stresses this part, we didn't care who saw or heard us. Things will be bad, very bad, without Amanda. He tells me that, and I know it to be true because I feel it myself. She is was our double-sided tape. He says he couldn't stop her, that she shot ahead and he found her a half mile away. There was a cluster of people around her body. He had to fight through them to see her. She was hit by a teenage boy driving a Jeep Cherokee. She must not have been looking while she ran.

It happened, he tells me. *That is what happens when you choose Circle Nine instead of staying here, where it's safe.*

I'm not going anywhere, Sammy, I say.

CHAPTER TWENTY-FIVE

Five-and-a-Half Weeks Before

Since Amanda died, it's as if I have been granted permission to see into another reality.

My thoughts are confused, disordered.

The world is sometimes perfect as it used to be, sometimes gray and bitter.

I can't sort it all out, so I sleep.

And sleep, and sleep.

That's what we have done for most of the past few days, Sam and me.

Today, though, Sam says we have to go. He says we have to pay our respects.

Pay our respects?

In Circle Nine. They stole her away. They have her now, but we can say good-bye.

Part of me is angry. Can we never be rid of Amanda? Because really, this is what I wanted—for her to disappear, so I can have Sam back, all mine, for good.

I want you there, he says. *It'll be fun. A day trip.* He knows I hate being here for too many hours on end.

We pull on rain gear. It's blustery and cold. These feelings are somewhat foreign to me; I used to notice them, but somehow they never touched me. I could feel the cold on my skin without feeling it sink deep below. It is as if a protective orb has always surrounded me until now.

I shiver as we step outside our home. Sam clasps my hand, and then we are off into the impenetrable world.

We crouch hidden behind an angry marble tomb many yards away from the crowd.

It's a mausoleum, Sam says.

Like for the Egyptians, I say back. Sam shakes his head. He ignores me. He clutches a colorful strand tight in his palm. It's one of her bracelets, one she always wore. The lucky one.

Where did you get it? I ask him.

She gave it to me, he says.

When? I press. Amanda wouldn't have given up the lucky one.

I took it, he admits. *When she died. Look, it's not like she needs it anymore.*

I nod. I try to stretch my legs out, but Sam stops me, puts a firm hand on one knee.

We have to stay hidden, or they'll see us, he tells me. *We'll get in trouble.*

I don't want to hide. I want to run up past the gravestones over the grass burst through this crowd of people we don't know jump into the wet soggy earth with Amanda. Who are these people who cluster around her? Who is that overweight man all in black patting that little boy's shoulder? Why are they here? Amanda was ours. We do not know these people.

I'm sad, Sammy. I rest my head on his shoulder, where I feel that he is tense.

Why?

Because she's gone.

She isn't gone, Abby, he says. *Amanda is not dead.*

I am confused, but I don't say anything. How can she not be dead? She can't talk to us anymore; she can't dance in circles or play word games or laugh or kiss Sam when I'm not looking or try to kiss me, too. My anger boils up. I can't think like this. There is no reason for me to think like this, now that she is gone.

Sam, I ask, *why are we here? Why do we need to see her again? We're OK on our own.*

She wanted to go to California, Abby, he says dreamily. *That's where she always wanted to go. Let's go to Cali just as soon as we can. We'll bring her with us.* He has tears in his eyes all of a sudden, and his voice sounds gruff. Rage flows through me at this. He can't love her. He doesn't. But maybe he did. Maybe he did love her all his life like she said. What does it mean? How could he love us both? Why is he trying to keep her alive? Why won't he let her go?

I never want to see Amanda again. I am a pillar of locusts and vultures and poison and everything bad. I think of her funeral pyre. She is now all burned up so she fits in a small metal jar. I wonder how it was done, if there was a special ceremony for that. I feel at once regretful that we missed it, happy she is gone, sad she is gone, and guilty for feeling happy at all. I am a big, fiery mix of emotions, a column of fire to match her own.

We wait there long after the Circle Nine people have gone, and they have dumped dirt in Amanda's hole. My legs are cramped and for a while, I take a nap in Sam's lap. When he nudges me to wake up, my body feels stiff and tired. It's long-dark, I can tell from the richness of the shade of black cloaking us. We walk to Amanda's hole and stare at it for a long time. Sam mutters words I can't understand. He paws at the earth.

Maybe she will need it, he says. *Maybe it is like the Egyptians. Maybe I shouldn't have taken it.* Sam digs and digs with his hands. He wants to give the bracelet back. Sam digs a tunnel to Amanda. I imagine him crawling through it, as if Amanda is China. My heart is thumping hard in my chest. But suddenly there is a noise and then a light, and we are running off into the night, finding pockets of darkness to conceal us. We are panting by the time we get back to the cave. Inside and outside, the world is a muddled mess of dim and dark and gray. Sam still has Amanda's bracelet tucked into his palm. When he opens his hand, I see that he's left crescent moons in his skin, he was gripping it so hard.

It's OK, he says, but it sounds like he's talking mostly

to himself. *It's OK. She wouldn't mind us having it. She wouldn't mind.* He carries the bracelet over to the corner and sets it carefully on a small ledge there. He rummages around the rest of the cave-palace. He returns with some of her things: some clothes she kept here, a toothbrush. He sets them by the bracelet.

A shrine, he explains. *She would have liked that. She liked attention.* He looks proud of himself, but I only feel sick. She will always be here. She invaded our space like locusts and won't ever leave, even in death.

CHAPTER TWENTY-SIX

Four Weeks Before

We are making dinner together, Sam and me. It has been so long since we've done it. Sam lights the stove, and I pour glasses of wine fuller than I should. We cook mutton and eat it together at a long oak table, where we sit on either side in high-backed thrones, far away from each other so we have to shout our conversation. The meal is delicious, and I am so happy because Sam is in a good mood. He is so rarely in a good mood anymore. Ever since Amanda ... but that is finished, and we don't speak of it.

Amanda's shrine is in the corner still, and we fixed her a plate, too, setting it carefully by her belongings. She hasn't touched it. Sam looks a little worried, but I can tell he is putting on a brave face because the atmosphere is so jolly and he doesn't want to ruin it. Afterward, we curl up together, drunk and full, and the cave is filled with our laughter, lit from within by a rainbow aura. It is like old times.

Yesterday, I had another one of my dreams. The same woman, the same girl. A man this time, too. They're getting clearer, and I can make out very specific facial features now, and so my sketches are more detailed than ever.

When I showed Sam my new sketch, he was enraged. I would not use that strong of a word unless I thought it were true. He tore it in half, and I nearly cried. I used to think he gets so angry because he is afraid I would leave him to try to find these other people. He must know that no one could take me away from him. But if he doesn't, it means he's afraid of something else. And so I can't help but think he might know something he isn't telling me. When he looked at my drawing, his face was ashen. Maybe Sam is right to be worried. After all, they are from Circle Nine.

His anger, though, makes me angry. Ever since Amanda died, my itch to know who I am has grown, as if the shock of her death brought something in me alive. The pain in my head doesn't stop me; I push through it, along with the danger of Sam's fury and of Circle Nine. I am hungry for clues. I suspect this angers him more than anything else. But after all, he hid my little journal so long ago. If he is hiding something else, I must find it. But along with these thoughts races a parallel line of thinking that shouts in my ear: no, no, you are betraying yourself by doubting him! He is your only ally. I don't know truth from anything else. I realize now that I never had a concept of truth, only of instinct. I must try to trust my instincts. There's just one thing I need to find out, above all else — even if my identity remains elusive, I need to find out who the people in my pictures are.

Why Amanda reminded me of Dream Girl. How it all connects.

I eye Sam from across the room, where I am dusting Amanda's shrine. (I like to keep it clean.) He is reading a book and writing in his journal. He is sitting in the leather chair, which has brass studs lining its bottom edges and arms, and his feet are propped up on our ottoman. He smiles at me, and I smile back quickly before I resume my polishing.

I am suspicious of Sam and the way he's been acting. I wish I could help it. I feel guilty. When I try, I can swat my suspicion away and not think about it. It's easiest when he's happy and we're like we used to be, like tonight. But even now, I think of it.

CHAPTER TWENTY-SEVEN

Four Weeks Before

This one was so awful that I wake up shaking with my mouth open in a wide-mouthed grimace because I'm unable to scream. I feel his arms tucking around me as he whispers *shhhh* into my ear.

What this time, baby?

Another fire, I gasp. *And two others.*

Who was it? Did you see them this time?

A man and a woman, Sammy. Dead. Their eyes were lifeless, their faces burned. They were wrapped all around each other, intertwined like we are now. They were dead, but then the woman reached out to me, made a grab for my hand. I looked into her eyes, and they were mine.

What do you mean, made a grab for you?

My wrist. But I was very small, just a little girl. Her fingers broke off where they touched me, crumbled to dust. I ran to a dark space under a cupboard and hid.

How old? He pets my hair.

Eight, maybe. Nine. Sammy, I think they were my parents. I think they didn't want me to leave.

No, baby. You and me, we don't have families.

Not anymore, you mean.

No. Never. That's why you can't remember anything before me. You've always belonged to me.

Then why do I dream these things? Who are these people? Who is that girl? I challenge him because something in me says I know different.

Was she there, too? His tone is sharp.

No! I say. *Just the other times. The times I've told you about.*

OK, he says soothingly. *Back to bed,* mija. *Forget all that.* Soon he is snoozing.

But forgetting has always been my trouble. I don't want to forget; I want to cling to these memories and dreams, which come nearly every evening now, much more often than I admit to Sammy. Something in me makes me hold back from him. They're more real to me when he can't just explain them away. They're more real than anything I've ever known. Sometimes, and then it scares me, they're more familiar to me than Sammy.

I don't know Sammy all the time anymore. I look at him sometimes and I see this foreign person, this being other than myself. He didn't used to be a separate being. He was as much of me as my arms and legs. Tearing him away, I used to imagine, would cause too much bleeding for me to stay alive. Now I think I could stay alive. But I wouldn't want to. I miss feeling sewn together, and the times I don't feel it I know I am more alone than anyone else in the universe. So I hold on to him as tight as I can.

Even so, the more I realize I could maybe survive without him, the more I turn toward these memory-gifts. And the more memories I invite in, the more my headaches improve; the pain in my head is a barrier that's crumbling, leaving me freer than before.

These changes tug at my world and make me fight with Sam and make things bad between us, and the dynamic shifts every time just slightly and I fight to get it back but it's so elusive. How could things have once been so perfect? I see the world now in all colors and shades of darkness and light, and the darkness mixes with the light until it's indiscernible, where before the only dark was outside our home and the only light within. Something awful has happened to change me. And with it came the girl with the black hair and these people, *my parents,* and they're poking their way into our home and my head. Nothing is safe from my nightmares. I am not safe; I don't know what is real and what is imagined. Sammy is my only voice of reason, but sometimes the darkness takes him away, too, and then I have only myself. I can feel a gap opening between Sam and me like when Amanda was around, but this one has nothing to do with jealousy. I will stop telling Sam about my dreams. I'll figure it out on my own.

CHAPTER TWENTY-EIGHT

Three-and-a-Half Weeks Before

It's been weeks of this mourning and not mourning *because Abby, she's still with us—don't you see? Soon we'll go out West and it'll be OK. All three of us! That's what she wanted; we'll give it to her.* And nervous agitation and nightmares, so I convince Sam to change things up. We can only take so much of our old routine, and everything feels stale now anyway. I once loved the long, languid hours of it, but now it only makes me sick with unease. My stomach has turned more nervous, and I'm always sick, sick with constant pains that keep me in the bathroom forever and because of it, my appetite has shriveled up into a walnut, old and weathered. I am desperate for change.

So I tug Sam's arm and whine until he agrees. We are to go to the cinema. The word is delicious in my mouth. He agrees and I am like a child! I am so excited. But there's also the thrill from the danger of it. We are going to the cinema, which is in Circle Nine, which of course is horribly dangerous. Sam hopes, I think, to drive away my restlessness with one night of recklessness.

I dress up sexy for the occasion. Amanda has left behind a black slinky something that isn't quite a dress, more a bandage that wraps my body tight to the thighs as if everything above that is one big sore it needs to protect. Sammy won't be able to see it much, though, because it's black night out, so my dress and the air around us and everything we see will blend into one black haze. That's why Sammy agreed, anyway. The cinema is a night thing we found out about in the layers of newspaper that wrapped our fresh fish dinner the other night. It was printed in ink: outdoor night cinema on the big screen, given by a local documentary film club—and the ink rubbed off on our fillet's underbelly as if we were meant to eat the headlines, too. And so Sammy has agreed because in the night we are more protected, and it is likely we will be safe from the horrible things that haunt Circle Nine in the day. Which is why we go for food and our other things we need mostly just in the night. And now our Date will be in the night, and we'll be like a normal couple, the kind we read about in Sam's novels. I hope the cinema will become a regular thing.

I slather on lipstick, the pink stuff, and put green sparkles on my eyes. Traces of Amanda on my face. When I am done my eyes match my peacock-feather boa. Sam looks at me and part of him smiles, but then he removes the boa and makes me wipe my lips on the fabric of his dark sweater, where the pink turns into nothing but a greasy smudge.

If you want to go unseen, he says, *you're hardly trying.*

I just got carried away.

Then we are walking through the trees for fifteen, twenty minutes until the trees break and we are on the border of a beautiful wide park. I can feel Sam's hopes for me waxing in every step. He thinks this film will cure me of my nightmares and make me docile again, content with only our little nucleus. But when I see the rows of people stretched out in an ocean before us, I am anything but. I am more intoxicated by Circle Nine, even if I am still frightened as ever. I pause.

Is this the same place as before? I ask him.

What do you mean, before?

Before. With the fire. Are we in the same town?

No. I feel Sam's hand clench mine tight. *We've left that place behind. We're somewhere different now. This is the town I go to for food sometimes. The town where Sid lives, you remember?*

But where? I only want to get my bearings.

North, Abby. North of there. Don't worry about it. Let's go before we're late.

Sam clutches my hand as I move forward, drawing me back toward the trees.

We stay here, he says. He points to a grouping of rocks just outside the trees, far back from the crowd. *Crowds are dangerous,* he reminds me. So we keep our distance.

As the film flickers on, there's nothing I can concentrate on so much as the people in front of me. They turn their attentions to the screen, but if I look closely, I can see more than that. There are girls scooted backward between their boys' legs, couples like Sam and me. And they curl into each other like we do. They don't look so dangerous.

There are groups of girls my age laughing with each other. There are picnic baskets spread at their feet, and they reach for cheese and crackers at the same time, brushing knuckles without taking their eyes off the screen. It's an intimacy I can't have with any girl. It's something I could never have had with Amanda, who was always too cunning to relax into me, threading her affection with mine like these girls do, even when we were getting along. It's something I think I might feel with the girl from my dreams.

I try to think about the movie and enjoy Sam because that is what I came here to do. It is our big Date. But somehow I feel sordid and sick again in my slinky dress and heels. The other girls are wearing jeans and cotton shirts and they look lovely, and it is I who is the ugly thing here, not Circle Nine. I make big efforts to stop thinking; thinking so much all the time is what Sam hates most about me. And so I bring my eyes to the screen. It is a documentary.

A selection of short films, Sam whispers in my ear. He has found a program which has drifted from somewhere along this summer breeze.

Which one are we on? I ask.

Birdcalls America, he says. I am transfixed for a while

as I watch a man in a kayak paddle across a long, wide stream, probably very dangerous, with creatures that would gobble him alive, in search of the elusive ivory-bellied woodpecker. He finds him without much trouble, although he's whispering most of the time so as not to disturb the bird, and so the camera doesn't pick up much of what he says and I barely know what's going on. Then after his victorious moment in which he wades across the stream (and I'm not so much frightened any-more as exhilarated) and snaps a shot of the woodpecker, and then becomes famous across bird-watching circles in America, the screen fades out.

Then on again.

The Forgottens: A Story of a Lost Youth.

I sit taller on my rock.

It is all about no ones, kids like Sam and me, without families or attachments. That's what we know.

But these kids were born with families who were ripped from them, either in tragic accidents or circum-stances they couldn't prevent, like poverty. Or maybe some were abandoned by parents who were sick.

Suddenly a flash enters my skull. It sears in pain. I am trembling. I can feel Sam go stiff beside me.

Let's go, he whispers.

No. I refuse. I stay put. He knows he can't yell because we are close enough to the people to cause a scene. So for once, I have my way.

The documentary is told in ministories that chronicle certain lost souls—orphans and street kids. After it's over, a melodramatic narrative voice bellows across the lawn from the sound system around us:

This film is dedicated to the loving memory of one of our own Winston County Documentary Film Club members who passed away tragically last year in a fire on Orchard Lane in Pineview.

As the voice continues in monotone, the camera pans to a neighborhood setting that looks vaguely familiar. Then a photo flashes across the screen: a pretty little dark-haired girl on a tire swing. It looks as if this will be a slide show, in memoriam. I see a date and the beginnings of a name, text that passes quickly under the photo, but before I can see the rest, Sam snatches my hand hard enough that I cry out, and though the sound is mostly muffled, I see some people turn. My arm might be pulled from my socket. Sam is on his feet, blocking the screen from view.

Stop, Sammy! I want to say, but I say nothing. I have never seen him look so monstrous.

We need to leave. Now. His tone is harsher than I've ever heard, and his eyes glow red, so I follow him because I am afraid.

But part of me feels urgently that I must stay here. I glance back to the screen, which is smaller behind me and partly obscured by the trees we are now dashing through. I am hurt and confused and something in me *needs to see who the dead girl was,* even though my head is begging for mercy.

†

When we get home, I face Sam in anger. He has ruined my date. Why do I have no choices? He catches his breath and pulls me to the floor, where he sits.

Abby, he says, *that film was evil. It will pollute your brain. And it was mediocre. We're above that, you and me. The people who made it must have been dumb. Infantile. Plebeian.* Sam shakes his head in apparent disgust.

But why, Sammy? Why was it so bad?

Everything about that place is bad, he says. *It disgusts me; it really does. You will become evil if you let it tempt you.*

I don't think it's so evil, I say. I am obstinate. *I think you make this up,* I say.

If you don't believe me, Abby, I can tell you this: you will lose me forever if you begin to desire Circle Nine.

I am silent; there is nothing more for me to say. It always comes down to that, and I can't argue. He knows I want that least of all, less than I want to explore the world. Our argument is over and Sam takes me tenderly in his arms, but I am still bothered. There was something about that film that seeped under my skin and became a dozen small worms wriggling there. I scratch all over. I need it out. I must find out. I need the truth now, and nothing can send me back to that oblivious state in which I was once happy. I will find out what happened to me, who I am, what came before this life with Sam, regardless of what Sam thinks. Regardless of how dangerous it may be.

CHAPTER TWENTY-NINE

Three Weeks Before

I know I must look a sight. Sam passed out cold again after a sleepless, tense night of pacing. When he passes out these days, I can usually count on an hour, maybe two before he wakes up. Leaving is a risk, but I had to try. It took me forty minutes to run through the woods. I don't have much time.

The librarian is eyeing me warily. I know all kinds of things about libraries, even though I don't know this particular one. I know it's where you go when you want answers. I know about the archives, where old newspapers are kept. I think I must have always known, even though I don't remember when or where I learned it. I think the things I carry with me—bits and pieces of Circle Nine knowledge—stay with me from Before because they have nothing to do with the big blanks of nothingness that are Me, my essence. I have lots of this kind of knowledge. The things I remember are the things I least crave to know.

I had to ask someone where the library was; I've only been in this town once before. I went right to the park, the park where we saw the film. I walked right up to one of those Circle Nine demons because I had to know.

Where is the library? I asked. The demon—it was a girl about my age, holding a baby—didn't look evil. Neither did the baby. But I know underneath it all, they're corrupt and teeming with sinister thoughts. I had to do it, though. I had to know about the library. She told me and then she looked at me strangely, as if there was something wrong with *me* instead of something wrong with *her*, but I guess that's what they do; and I hurried away. She didn't follow. But I'm still feeling a chill.

Do you have anything about a fire on Orchard Lane? I ask the librarian. The street name is the only bit of information I have to go on.

The librarian clucks her tongue. *My, what a tragedy that was,* she says. She turns her back on me and begins clicking on her computer, scrawling notes with one hand as she squints at the screen. My mind wanders; I am getting anxious. I don't know how I know how to speak to the librarian, why the musty shelves feel warm and comfortable instead of unfamiliar. As far as I remember, I have never been here before. Yet I am beginning to get used to this curious déjà vu, this instinctual knowledge I seem to possess. I know I must have been here, or somewhere like this, Before. I fight to remember, but I can't. The librarian clears her throat, and I jump. She's looking at me oddly. *Are you OK?* she asks. I nod and take the index card she's extending toward me.

Reference, it reads in her neat print. 4th floor. 4.10.1791. She taps her finger on the last number. *This is the code — four for fourth floor, ten for Reference, 1791 for order of the periodical. Let me know if you need any help.*

Thanks, I say. She nods back. Her face is still distorted into something wondering. I hope she doesn't get too curious, start asking questions. Suddenly the gravity of what I've done hits me: I'm *in* Circle Nine. Fully here, on enemy land. Any wrong word or motion might betray us. And there'd be no chance for escape. Someone asking questions could mean someone following me back could mean Sam and I are separated, forced to live somewhere apart. All because we are too young. Sam has always been right. This place is frightening — the power of everyone in it overwhelming — especially without him.

I duck my head as I walk away, toward the elevator, old and creaky. When I reach the fourth floor, it takes me a few minutes to locate the reference section. It's quiet in here, so quiet I'm spooked. I estimate it's been almost an hour already. If Sam sleeps for two, I might have fifteen or twenty minutes left. I pray he sleeps for two. If he finds out I came out alone, in the middle of the day . . . I shudder at the possibility.

When I get to Reference, I see a stack of papers a mile high. I panic. She forgot to write down the date. There are a week's worth of papers in this stack. I feel the hopelessness of it. But I begin thumbing through them frantically, anyway. I'm not even sure where to look, so I just glance at the headlines.

It's been ten minutes and I'm losing hope because I only have ten left, max, and I came all this way and I refuse to go home with nothing. I am shocked at my own boldness, but at the same time my nerves are on over-drive. I accidentally drop some of the papers, and I jump at the sound they make, even though it's soft, as they hit the floor. I'm gathering them up again when I see it:

Blaze on Orchard Lane Pending Investigation

Four locals are reported missing following a fire that destroyed their home last Monday. The fire, which authorities believe originated in the master bed-room, quickly turned one family's two-story home into an uncontrollable inferno.

"Any bodies would have been reduced to ash," said Fire Chief Jim Wexel. "A fire like that, there was nothing we could do."

Although evidence does not point to arson, the cause of the fire is still pending investigation.

Chills crawl up my spine as I read. The article is sad; it is a horrible thing to have happened to a family. Part of me wonders if I am connected to this at all—it seems far-fetched. It occurs to me that Sam really did just want to protect me from seeing the ugliness of the world, like he says. That he just wanted to keep Circle Nine from hurting me, like he always does. That makes far more sense than the idea that I'm somehow connected to a local tragedy. But memories of the night I met Sam flash through my mind. The charred building, the heat on my face, the sirens in the distance. I'm cold all over.

I must get home to Sam. Maybe I can find a way to ask him about it, so this will all be cleared up without me having to sneak around. But not just yet. Something tells me to keep my secrets just a little while longer. I'll ask Sam when I have more of a reason to think that there's a link between me and this fire. Something to prove I'm not just imagining things. For now, it'll be my secret. Every girl needs her secrets. This is something I'm learning late.

My heart thuds a little harder as I realize I'm probably behind schedule, that Sam might be awake and waiting for me — or worse, looking for me, worried. I gather up all the papers in a stack, except this one. I take a quick look around and, when I'm convinced there's no one up here, I quietly tear out the article and shove it in my back pocket. I hide the mangled paper in the middle of the stack. If the librarian somehow were to find out, that would be the end of my research. I must come back. I must find a way to have more time to myself. But how, during the day? Sam is nearly always around lately. He never even goes to Sid's anymore. Poor Sammy, always sick and listless. But how can I capture more than two hours for myself?

I promise myself to figure it out later. For now, getting back there before he wakes up is the only important thing. I run down the stairs instead of waiting for the elevator and as I'm darting past the front desk, the librarian calls out to me, *Do you need anything else, honey?* And the way she says it shoots warning signs into my brain, but I shake my head and wave and keep going anyway, hoping she'll pass this off as one other weird thing that happened in her day, just one more crazy teenager.

Then I'm off, faster than before. I dart through town and into the woods behind the high school like a gazelle. I run around trees, over stones, until the paths bordering the property thin out and give way to dense foliage. I know these rocks and trees so well by now; it couldn't be easier if they wore labels.

Then I am back, bending over my knees, my chest heaving, and as I catch my breath and walk into our home, I see him stirring a little at the sound of my footsteps.

Abby? he says groggily, *What are you doing?*

Nothing, honey, I say. *Did you have a nap?*

Yeah, he says. He struggles to sit up but clutches his head. *I have the worst headache.*

Is there anything I can do, Sam-Sam? I am struggling to keep my voice even, since I'm still catching my breath.

I don't think so, babe. I don't know. He pauses, as if considering something. Then, *No there's nothing.*

So I bring him some water from the brook, wet on a T-shirt, and use it to blot his forehead, which is sopping and coal-hot. My poor Sam. I usually tell him everything, but this time, this one time, I can't. I am guilty over it all night.

CHAPTER THIRTY
Two-and-a-Half Weeks Before

Tell me how beautiful I am, I say. It is our old game, and I want to resuscitate it. It is a rare day today; Sam is well and in a good place. We're outside and there's a slight chill in the air and we're lying on dirt and leaves that crinkle under our bodies but somehow feel soft at the same time. And when the chill's too much and my skin begins to pimple up, Sam hugs me close. It's perfect out here, lovely and serene. Sam is more handsome than I ever remember seeing him. I take a deep breath and hold it for as long as I can. As long as I can hold it in, none of this goodness can escape. Things feel so normal, so good, that I give in to my urge to forget everything that's been happening to us. Sam's poor health and the dangerous hunger for knowledge that propelled me into Circle Nine three days ago. I need this peaceful time with him. I dunk my body in his words and swim around in them, drinking them close to my heart.

How can you not know how beautiful you are? You are more beautiful than life, he says. I can tell he means it, but I push him further.

That's nothing, I scoff. *Life is hideous.*

OK, he says, starting over. *You're lovelier than the rocks that jut out into the sea on the coast of France. You're lovelier than the way the water crashes against them and sprays its mist on my toes.*

You don't know that, I challenge. *You've never even been to the coast of France.*

Haven't I? he asks. *How can you be so sure?*

Well, what about this? I say. I roll over on my hip and point to a dimple in my thigh.

That? he asks, surprised. *That is pure joy. That is innocence. It's a baby's smile. What could make me happier?* He caresses it as if it's something to be treasured.

OK, then, this. I grasp the left side of my chest in my palm and nudge it upward to show him. The left side is smaller than the right, lopsided. There is no beauty in that.

He laughs. *Oh, you think you're clever,* he says. *You think because I am a guy, I won't love all of you. Well, let me tell you a story.*

I roll my eyes. Somehow, my stunted left breast invited a story. But I listen anyway—that's the rules of the game.

Once, he begins, *there was a tiny duckling. His feathers were scraggly, and he never outgrew his newborn fuzz tufts. His beak was nothing to brag about. His siblings, though—now, they were something else.*

Stop! I say, laughing. *You're telling me "The Ugly Duckling"? You're actually likening my breast to the ugly duckling?*

Oh, you know it? He seems genuinely surprised.

Of course I do, I say. But then I wonder, as I do with all things like this, why I'm so sure and where I've heard it before. It's one of those strange things I just know.

Well, then, I'll have to be more creative, he says, taking my hand. He can tell my confusion bothers me. Sam is always able to read my thoughts.

Once, he says, starting yet again, *there was a tiny particle of fungus. Actually, I am not too sure what he was—some molecule or another. He was unpopular and nearly anonymous, as you can tell from the fact that I don't even know his name. We'll call him Louis.*

Louis? Why Louis?

The name suits him. Stop interrupting me.

I roll my eyes.

So, Lou just carries on for many years—centuries, really, like most bacteria and molecules and scientific stuff do, until one day, someone discovers him. Lou isn't thrilled, because he's come to like his anonymity. He's comfortable. He has a niche. No one pays much attention to him, but that's OK with him. So then someone discovers him, and he's all hot and bothered. Not to mention, he has a serious *inferiority complex.*

Sam nudges my leftie, and I giggle.

So when he's almost totally given up on himself and settled entirely for this life of nothingness, he's all of a sudden plucked out of nowhere. He's prodded, he's experimented with, he's basically lavished with attention, and he doesn't necessarily like it at first. But then . . . something special happens.

What happens?

Well, someone takes the time to really study him. To look at him, admire the attributes everyone else ignored. A little time goes by, and magic happens. Lou and his little fungus friends become . . . He pauses, watching my face.

Yes, Sam? I say to encourage him. He's all about the drama of the storytelling.

They become penicillin.

What? I am incredulous. *That's ridiculous,* I say. *You're not even using the correct terminology.*

You're missing the point. Anonymous, lonely, undervalued Louis becomes penicillin.

So you're saying my left breast is an antibiotic.

I'm saying it is capable of big things.

You're ridiculous, I say again. Then he's on me, all over me, kissing and tickling until I'm yowling and laughing so hard I almost pee and I'm begging him to stop. There's a warm glow surrounding us that I want to hold on to. And Sam's feeling well, and when he's well, his energy transfers right over to me and makes it impossible to think anything's bad. I want to have this silly, smart boy forever, but moments like these are so few now. I need these moments back, and just one, having just one every now and then makes me think I can have them all back again, every day. Sam helps me forget the library. He helps me forget what it is I wanted to discover. Most of all, he helps me forget that I've already forgotten so much, way too much.

CHAPTER THIRTY-ONE
Two Weeks Before

Again he sleeps. Sam is no longer a walking, breathing human. He is an automaton, a shadow. His basic functions have changed from a pattern of sleeping, eating, moving, loving, to sleeping, crying, retching, sleeping. It's getting harder to see him as fascinating or handsome these days. Every now and then I trick myself into it, but then a day passes, and the magic fades. I hate the way things have changed. Nothing I see is quite right anymore. I miss my Sam, the Sam I have loved all this time. I want him back. Sometimes he has good days, but they no longer outweigh the bad. I hate seeing him like this. I pray that he will recover.

But I don't think long about sneaking out as soon as he's fallen asleep. He sleeps longest and heaviest in midday. As soon as his breathing becomes steady and deep, as soon as the sheets have stopped rustling from the movements of his body, I slip on my jacket and step out onto sopping grass pelted by a drizzling sky. Everything is gray, so gray, and it is the perfect color to describe my present state. If only I could pick a color each day to slip in front of my eyes and change not only my vision but my perception. The world I'm jogging through no longer seems quite as murky and dangerous as it once did. As I run, I watch the foliage that borders our home begin to thin into a smattering of trees. And then I'm behind the high school and its yellow cement blocks and heavy columns, with the knowledge that only seven blocks away is a small brick building that holds all the answers.

It seems no coincidence that the more I venture out alone, the less afraid I am. But then that is the most frightening part of Circle Nine, according to Sam: it is quietly deceptive. It lures you in by seeming familiar, comfortable. And by the time you realize you've been duped, it's too late to turn back. That, says Sam, is why I must stay away from this world at all costs. I know there's danger in what I'm doing, but I'm drawn to it anyway, as though I am the moth and Circle Nine is the flame. I wonder if there's always such danger in seeking the truth.

Turn back. Run from Circle Nine before it's too late. That is what my brain tells me. It's what I've learned to think from the person I love and trust. But what about my instincts? *Trust, but be wary,* they say. Anyway, I no longer have a choice. The hunger for truth has driven me this far, away from Sam despite the cost, and with each step I take, I grow more famished. It is beyond my will to turn back now.

The same librarian is sitting at the reception desk when I walk in. She clucks her tongue disapprovingly as I pull off my coat, spraying water over the floor.

There's a coatrack there. She nods in the direction of the rack. It's busier today; I'll have to be more careful, no page tearing this time. A mother sits with her little girl in one corner; what looks like a textbook is open in front of them. The girl pores over the book, making notes in the margin. I am suddenly and painfully aware of the void in my heart.

Miss? The librarian is speaking to me. *Miss, do you have a library card?*

I shake my head. All I want is to get upstairs to the fourth floor, and fast.

Well, have you thought about getting one?

I shake my head again, and she peers at me suspiciously, as if I have no right to be here.

Go on, then. You just can't check out any books today. I am already rushing to the elevator, jamming my finger over and over on the button marked *4*, shifting from side to side as I bear the interminable wait. The elevator is one of those old-fashioned types, with a door that swings open to reveal a gate, which one must pull back in order to step in. It takes me another long minute to remember the door's not automatic. Then I'm up, up, and away, the feeling of promise tingling all over.

The stack is just as I left it: in a state of mild disarray. I quickly locate the page I ripped. I flip around a little more at random but don't come up with anything. It briefly crosses my mind that the story would have made the national news, but I dismiss that as unlikely. Tragedy in a small town isn't likely to draw national attention. And even if it did, it probably got more local coverage than national. I flip back through the stack, combing every page of the papers dated all the way through two, then three weeks prior to the one I found already. But there's nothing. There *must* have been some coverage, something coming before my article! I flip through again, more carefully this time, but the papers are void of any mention of the fire on Orchard Lane. It's almost as if . . .

The thought is insane, but I can't help considering it. It's almost as if someone else was here before me. As if someone else got rid of them. I massage my temples, which have begun to pound. The thought is ridiculous; no one knows me except Sam. And Sam doesn't know that I've been here, and he couldn't have known I was coming. I feel as if I am losing my mind. Then I remember. The article I found had mentioned a coroner's report. I hadn't thought to look forward, only back. I grab the stack and frantically flip forward.

Everything all right?

I jump. The voice has startled me. A lanky boy about my age with blond hair and retro glasses is standing in front of me. I pull myself up from my crouch; my knees are unsteady.

Yes, fine, I say sharply. I instantly feel alarmed.

I'm sorry, he says. *Didn't mean to scare you. You just looked a little . . . intense.*

I'm fine, I say again.

Are you sure? he asks. *Because, you know, I could be of service.* He gives me a little crooked smile. Something inside me goes hot. Why is he talking to me? Is he . . . flirting?

Really, I say. *I just want to be alone.*

The boy gives me a disappointed nod, accompanied by another little smile, which I notice is sort of attractive. Then he walks away. I immediately feel bad for snapping. And guilty for noticing his smile. Maybe he wasn't flirting, I reassure myself. Maybe he really was just trying to be helpful. Maybe I was his good deed for the day. Or maybe, and at this next thought I tense up, maybe he recognizes me for who I am: someone panicked and fearful. Someone who steals from a library. Maybe, just maybe, he's involved in all of this, too. Maybe he knows something.

I really am going crazy. A boy flirts, and suddenly it's a conspiracy.

I kneel back down on the floor. I should not have snapped at the boy. If I look volatile, I'll look strange. If I look strange, people will ask questions. Then I see it.

I gasp. I am holding an article with an accompanying photo.

The photo in my hand is beyond déjà vu; I *know* it. But I don't know how.

I know this girl in the photo. I trace her face with one finger. My heart is beating faster now, so fast I feel I might pass out. *Who is this girl?* The long black hair, the black bangs. The piercing in one eyebrow.

Dream Girl.

She looks just like Dream Girl, just like my sketches. I read the article below the photo. It is dated July 12.

Shady Ridge High School will be holding a memorial service on Tuesday for 18-year-old Katherine James, a May graduate, and her younger sister, Addison James, who had just completed her sophomore year. Both girls are believed to have perished in the July 8 house fire that also claimed their parents: 47-year-old Justin James, a locally respected handyman, and his wife, 42-year-old Luanne James.

The service is open to the public and will be held in the high-school gymnasium at 4 pm.

I feel overwhelmingly sick. The shot is a professional one, possibly a high-school graduation photo. Her luminous smile radiates warmth, and nothing about it is affected or posed. This is a girl who was open and honest. A girl who was happy. And that's when I notice her necklace, a thin gold chain barely peeking out from below her yellow blouse, holding a piece of gold script just at her clavicle. I might not recognize it if I didn't know it so well.

It is just like mine.

I reach up to my own throat, fingering the necklace that lies there. I peer closely at the photo. *Katie,* said hers. *Abby,* says mine. There must be a million girls with these same gold necklaces. But something inside me *knows* that this is not a coincidence. This can't all be a coincidence. But there was no Abby in the article; there were only two girls, and the second was Addison. My heart sinks; I realize I *wanted* to be Dream Girl's sister. I'd felt certain these people I dreamed were mine. I wanted it all to make sense; I wanted to be the fourth. But maybe all along, I was connected in some other way. An outsider, just a friend.

But I feel closer than that. I look down at my Abby necklace again. Maybe I am trying too hard to make everything fit. I feel so close; I'm desperate and perplexed.

This time, Sam's sitting at the dining table when I arrive home, out of breath. It's as if Circle Nine has followed me back and is eager to transpose its own images on the ones I usually see; for a moment, the dining table looks like an upside-down crate, a thin piece of cardboard covering its surface. Sam himself looks skeletal. Then I close my eyes hard, and when I open them, everything's normal again. Except Sam; he still looks gaunt and wasted. These inconsistencies — these blips where my eyes betray me — have been happening ever since Amanda died. I am losing my head.

Sam glares at me. His arms are folded.

Don't try to tell me you were outside in the creek, he says through gritted teeth.

*I—I—*My words stick in my throat. I don't know what to say.

Don't lie to me, Abby, he says again. I have no choice.

I was at the library, I tell him.

Doing what? His words are steel.

Researching, I say. *Researching Orchard Lane.*

And why would you be doing that? Now his voice is cruel, mocking.

It's not a coincidence, Sam. I can feel it. The dreams, the way you pulled me away at the cinema. I can hear my voice rising. It is laced with desperation. If he were on my side, this would be so much easier.

What did you find. He says it like it's a statement.

This old photo today, it looked just like my Dream Girl! It looked like this girl I've been drawing! I run to the wall and rip one of my drawings down to show him. *And Sam,* I continue, *she was wearing a necklace just like mine!*

SHUT UP! he shouts. His hands are clutched over his ears. *Noise—it's all this noise—just shut up already!*

My eyes have already begun to fill, but I don't cry, as I usually would. He's grabbing me by the shoulders and shaking me now.

Don't you see, Abby? You're crazy. You're one-hundred-percent, bat-fucking crazy, and I didn't want to have to be the one to tell you that, but it's true! You're making all this stuff up in your head!

I shake my head no, tears falling down my cheeks. No. It can't be like that. I'm not crazy. I know I'm not. I am all emotion. I am all these things I want to push away. I try to regain control, but I can't—there is nothing left but panic and pain.

Yes, he says. *Why didn't I let you see the film at the cinema? Because I was afraid you were too weak to handle seeing that kind of sadness, Abby! Because you're not strong like the rest of us! And why does that girl from the photo look like Dream Girl? Well, who else does she look like, Abby? Who? Tell me!*

Amanda, I whisper.

That's right. When did you start having those dreams? After *Amanda came. Because you were so obsessed with Amanda and so jealous of her!*

No, I say. *That's not it.* Fight, a fight to stay calm. A fight to stay in control of my thoughts.

Oh, give it up, he says. *You've created this big fantasy in your head about some prior existence where you had a family and things were all rosy. Some horrible tragedy where you were the victim. But guess what, Abby? When I found you lying there that night, you were so high you didn't know who you were! You probably OD'd! If you want to know the truth,* that's *probably why you can't remember anything. You were just a little ratty street kid who happened to wind up in the wrong spot, nothing more. You were lucky I decided to take you in.*

It can't be true. I have never, would never, use drugs. But there he is; his mouth is foaming and his words are venom. Sam has never been so cruel. But perhaps I've been stupid to ignore the reality. Maybe he's right. Maybe this is all some construct of my imagination. His words have crushed my soul.

I'm telling you one last time. If I find out you've gone out alone again, we're finished. And then, Abby, he continues, drawing out this last sentence, *where will you go?*

He's right. I have nowhere to go. Sam lies down on Amanda's old bed tonight, and it's a cruel punishment for what I've done. My heart is in shreds, and my stomach is so sick that I know it will be impossible to fall asleep if I let things be as they are. I try to believe what he's saying. I thought that all I wanted was to have that old peace back, to share a life with him again in oblivion and be blissfully happy, as I used to be. I suppose that kind of happiness can't ever last. But here I am, in the trenches of hell, darkness seeping into my skin.

A half an hour goes by before I approach him.

Sam? The whites of his eyes blink acknowledgment in the dark.

Sam, I'm sorry, I say. *But I just needed to find out who I was. I feel sometimes like you try to hide it from me. Maybe I misunderstood. I'm sorry for what I did, but I just felt that I had to.*

When I am finished talking, I watch Sam's jaw clench several times, and he lies there unresponsive for a minute before I realize my error. I used the word *but.* I apologized, then tried to justify my apology. I have probably made him even angrier. I take a deep breath and try again.

Sam, I'm sorry for disobeying you, I say. *I'm sorry for sneaking out behind your back.*

Silence.

I'm sorry, I repeat, more fervently this time. *I'm sorry for what I did, Sam.*

I am met with more silence. My throat begins to fill up with a big, hurting ball.

Why are you ignoring me? I say. My voice has become louder and shriller. *Don't you have anything to say?*

No, I don't. He closes his eyes as if to go back to sleep, but I am in a panic. I cannot go back to sleep when he is treating me like this. I have done everything I can to make up for what I did. It isn't fair that I should be punished the way he is punishing me. I won't let him sleep.

Sam, I say, *I apologized. I said I am sorry. Why are you ignoring me like this?*

I'm not ignoring you. I'm waiting for a sincere apology.

I already apologized three times! I was *sincere!*

Oh, yeah? I'm sorry, but . . . he mimics me in a cold voice.

Sam, please, please just let it go. Why do you want to make this worse? I am crying now.

Oh, I'm not trying to make things worse, Abby. I want a sincere apology, then this can be over.

Sam, I am sorry, I say in a voice of stone.

That's supposed to be sincere?

I'm SORRY, I repeat more loudly. The words are muffled by the thick pain in my throat.

Sam shakes his head in disgust.

Why are you doing this? I say again. *Like you never do anything wrong? I did something wrong, and I apologized! That should be enough!*

I can feel frustration and anger flooding my body. Now it's more than just what I did. Now it's about what he's doing to me, too. Suddenly, it becomes blindingly clear: Sam is trying to control me. Sam *is* controlling me, has been controlling me all along. But it's so far gone that I can't figure out how to get myself out from under him. The only thing to do would be to leave him. These thoughts move in and out of my brain at a rapid pace. I feel sick, and also devastated.

I do things wrong now? When's the last time I did something wrong? Please, enlighten me. Tell me all about it.

I struggle to think, but my brain produces nothing.

I don't remember exactly, I say lamely. *But I know it's happened.* He laughs loud and cruel.

Now you're making things up. You're twisting things around just so you can make yourself feel better. Pathetic, Abby.

I'm not making anything up!

Oh, yeah? Well, then, what are you talking about?

I don't know, I cry, clutching my head now. *I can't remember it, but I know you've hurt me. I know you make me feel small and broken all the time!*

You're speaking in generalizations. You're making things up, he snarls. *You're not even speaking logically anymore.*

I am not making anything up! I shout. *Stop trying to manipulate me! Stop trying to make me believe my mind doesn't work!* He stares at me with a mixture of superiority and disgust. I am hurting so much inside. I don't care anymore about standing up for myself. I only want all of this to go away.

Sam, I beg, *please end this.*

If you had apologized sincerely from the beginning, none of this would have happened, he says.

What more do you want from me? I beg. An animal anger is taking hold of me. I feel crazed, uncontrollable. *What more do you want?* I shout the words over and over again. He is sitting up in the bed, now, so calm, so cold.

I only want an apology.

I'm SORRY! I shout again. *I'm sorry I'm sorry I'm sorry*

I'm sorry. I get down on my knees next to the bed. I clutch my hands together in a gesture of penitence. *I am sorry,* I say in this position. *Sam, I am sorry for everything I have done.* I feel the tears streaming down my face, and I feel his cold disinterest. Nothing is enough.

Something inside me snaps. I feel like a snake, then a panther. I hiss and growl accordingly. I am empty, hungry, possessed. I climb up on the bed and gnash my teeth. I get right up in his face, so my nose almost touches his, and I spit my apology.

Get away from me right now, he says through gritted teeth. Then, when I don't move right away, *You're crazy. There's something wrong with you.*

I know that the only thing wrong with me is this feeling of helplessness inside. This thing that tells me I can't do anything to change what is going on. That there is no point in keeping calm; for all my efforts, I have nothing to show. I can't blame him for producing this awful rage in me, but what would anyone do? What does a caged animal do before it resigns itself entirely to its fate?

I cry and cry and cry at the foot of his bed, until I am defeated enough to say, *I'm sorry, Sam. Nothing you have done can excuse my behavior. It was wrong and deceitful. And no matter what I felt or why I did it, it doesn't make it right.*

He stares at me for a long minute, gauging my

sincerity. All he can possibly see in my eyes is devastation, because there is nothing left in me but that. *Fine.* He nods. Then he rolls back over as if to go to sleep.

Fine?

Yes, you apologized. Now it's over. Fine.

Fine? Just like that? That's all you have to say?

What else would I say?

It isn't even about this anymore, I say. *What about everything that just happened in between my first apology and now?*

Well, you weren't giving me a real apology, he says. *I was waiting for one, then you blew up.*

What about the way you manipulated me? What about how you tried to control me?

And how did I do that, Abby?

I try to explain, but I find myself fumbling for words. I can't remember what he said, verbatim, to achieve those things.

You're making things up again. You're lying.

You were cruel.

I was not cruel. You were hysterical. I did nothing wrong. You exaggerate. You make things up to make yourself feel better.

I am not crazy, I say. *Sam, can you look inside your heart and say you had nothing to do with this? That you did nothing wrong?*

Yes, he says, settling back on his pillow. I stare at him. My shock courses through my veins. I had thought, that at this point, he would do his part. He would acknowledge his mistakes. I had thought that if I gave him what he wanted, he would be fair.

Sam, I whisper, nearly choking on the words, *I can't be with you.* I feel sick even as I say it. But it's what I have to do. What other choice do I have?

Well, then, I guess there's nothing more to say, he says.

I stare at him for a long while. It's as if he never cared about me at all. I can't take back what I said. But I'd expected more of a fight from him. When it doesn't come, I'm not sure I care. I feel hollow.

Then he speaks.

I'm sorry for calling you crazy, he says. *I shouldn't have said that. But you are crazy, when you get up in my face like that. It's not you anymore. You are crazy.*

I stare at him. This is almost unbelievable. Time immeasurable before he speaks again. *You're crazy sometimes, but I need you. I need you, Abby. I don't know what I'd do if I were alone.* It isn't much, but I decide to take it.

Thank you, I say. Then I roll next to him so our bodies are side by side and put my hand in his. I can see the outline of tears on his cheeks, the only evidence that he isn't as cold as he pretends to be. I wish I could feel compassion for him, but the argument has drained me. I feel as if I am betraying myself by staying. But the thought of being alone . . . it's too frightening to conceive of.

We used to cuddle, he says in his little-boy voice, so starkly opposite to the inhuman voice he used mere minutes ago. I roll over on my side and nestle my cheek in the crook of his chest and shoulder, wrapping my other arm over his ribs. He is so much less strong than I remember. Skinnier than I thought. When everything is falling apart, this is what it feels like: skin and bones and nothingness and defeat.

Thank you, he whispers. I kiss his chin in response.

Sam, I say just as my own eyes begin to droop, *what would make you happy again?* He takes a while before answering. I am wondering if somewhere, deep down, he wants me to leave as much as I think I should.

To know that we're all right, he says. *That's all I want.* His words betray the truth I've been suspecting and discarding, the thing I'm most afraid to believe — that in fact, Sam is as weak as I am. We fall asleep cradling each other. We are just two humans in all of this, at the mercy of the world around us. I wonder what it will take for us to be all right. I am surprised to find I'm not sure if I even want that. This fight has broken me, but it's also woken me up. I'm not strong enough to say good-bye. My mind is still confused, cluttered with warring images and perspectives that shift and change as if I have no jurisdiction over my own mind. But I've gained some small piece of power by saying I would. I fall asleep knowing that right now, I am fine, but in the morning, my mind will likely deceive me yet again. My memory is so fleeting. When Sam called me crazy, I believed him. As long as my brain is unfaithful, I have no hope for a life without him.

CHAPTER THIRTY-TWO
Ten Days Before: I have a memory.

It's a bad day for me. When I woke, my mouth was dry, my body was stiff, and my head was pounding like it had a mallet inside. My stomach growled long and searching. Something had happened, something terrible, but I couldn't right away quite recall what. Sam and I were curled up on Amanda's cot. Something intangible lay between us, and even as he kissed my cheek, I felt his reluctance. Then it all came back, soaking me with a sickened feeling.

Are you still upset? I asked him.

No, babe, he replied. *We're fine now.* But the effort it took for him to show affection betrayed him.

These are the things I know:

—The thing that happened between us last night was hideous.

—It has left a nasty aftertaste in my mouth, my head, and all over my body.

—Sam won't talk about it, even if I ask him. For him, it is over; for me, it lingers all over like a thick layer of filth.

—Sam makes me wary. I can't fully trust him.

And the things I want:

—I want my mind to be steady and strong.

—I want those days back from when Sam and I were happy.

—I want to know who I am, though it frightens me.

—I want something solid.

I wander again to my old reservoir of hope and escape. I pick up my pencil and sketch the face that comes to me mechanically by now; it's the one thing my hand knows how to draw anymore. I trace the curves of her cheekbones, the fullness of her lips, the roundness of her eyes. And as I'm tracing, my chin rests on my other hand. The point of my chin becomes the point of her chin. I shade in her narrow nose as I slide my finger gently over the slope of my own.

And then I realize it, and it comes to me so easily I could laugh.

The reason, one of the reasons, at least, that this girl looks familiar—she looks just like me. There are the familiar feelings of fear when I see it, but I keep looking, keep realizing, keep admitting. Push through all of it for the truth.

It's been so long since I've looked in a mirror. But by now I know the nuances of my face and what it feels like, what my features would look like if translated to paper. The one striking difference, I think, would be the hair. Her hair in the pictures I draw, and in the newspaper photo that I believe is her, too, is a long and unruly black. It sweeps over her shoulders untamed, as if she hasn't even tried to train it into something seemly. My own hair is a short blond shag. It's stick straight and messy. It's grown out a little over the weeks, chin-length now instead of boy-short like it was when I first met Sam. But it's different, nevertheless. I watch as a strand of it falls onto the paper below me. Yellow on black.

I'm thrust into the memory so quickly that I don't have time to brace myself or doubt its validity. I'm thrust past the pain that always warns me fierce in my head.

Oh, sweetie, *she says.* Trust me on this one. *The older girl is standing over the sink, running water over her cascades of blond, wavy hair. The hair I've always been so jealous of. It's thick and lovely, a sharp contrast to my thin, blond mop that I keep short for lack of anything else to do.*

Now, hand me that box, *she says. At first I resist.*

Don't do it! *I say.* You're already beautiful. You'll spoil it.

Oh, stop being so melodramatic. We all need a change once in a while. *She winks at me. I am in awe of her bravery. She's always been the brave one, the outlandish one, the one who can make people cower. She's dazzling. And I am meek, weaker. Just as beautiful, everyone says, but lacking in the charm she's full of. I reluctantly hand her the small, thick box. The box has all kinds of warnings on its side:* keep away from eyes; rinse thoroughly. *It promises a* true color. *But it doesn't promise what I know Katie wants: the thrill of a new identity. For some reason the thought of it—this little change—makes me panicky. I've never liked change; it shakes you up in all kinds of ways you can't foresee.*

Now, come on—help me out, *she says, and I reach for the tube of cream and begin smoothing it over her hair with the small, makeshift brush that came with it. We bought two boxes in case there wasn't enough. Her hair is so thick; she's got twice as much as the average girl. I layer the cream with bits of foil. There's no going back now.*

I understand why she wants to do it. Sometimes I'm sick of my own skin, too. But lately she's been doing things that are weird, unlike her. Her nose ring, her eyebrow ring, and now the hair. In school, I learned that sudden and dramatic changes to one's physical appearance are signs of depression. But no way is she depressed. She's effervescent.

We wait an hour before rinsing it all out. And then we do, and I am staring at a different girl. She's a hard-edged, badass, superwoman version of her former self. She was right; it's even better than before. Not for the first time, I am totally and completely filled with awe.

She giggles as she drapes her long black mane in front of my face. You like?

It's gorgeous, *I say. I mean it. I could never be this beautiful. Envy wriggles nasty inside of me like a worm.*

She giggles again. Always so serious! *She settles onto my lap and puts her bony arms around my neck. I look into the mirror opposite the cold, ceramic toilet where we're sitting.*

Her long black hair against my short blond shag makes a startling contrast. I can't help it; my heart swells with the beauty and shame of it.

Love you, *I say with a quick kiss to her cheek, making up for the twinge of vile resentment that I'm sure she can see; I've never hidden my feelings well. But she's oblivious. She leaps off me and swats me on the shoulder.*

Stop being so sentimental, sheesh. Over a little hair dye. *She shakes her head at me.* Now let's go show it off, see how the boys like it. . . . *And then she's sashaying out of the room, and I'm following, and we leave the house on the pretext of stirring up some excitement. There's always excitement with her. She knows how to make something from nothing. She may outshine me, but I feel lucky to bask in her glow.*

Heeeeey-ay, *says a skinny black boy in the street, whistling appreciatively as we walk by. She's really working it now, strutting her stuff.*

No, thank you, *she calls back to him.* I prefer my thugs buff. *I elbow her in the ribs. So inappropriate. She gets away with way more than she should. Then we're jogging off as the boy yells things behind us.* You're not *that* pretty, *he says, and we're laughing all the way. I want to hold on to her, like this, forever.*

I snap out of the memory nearly as quickly as I fell into it, and I'm shaking from its vividness. I'm light-headed and weak, though my headache fades quickly, much more so than usual. Now I know with certainty that no matter what Sam says, something is connecting me to this girl in the picture, and maybe to the girl who died in that fire. The similarities between the photo I saw and my drawings are too pronounced to be merely coincidental. I was close to this girl once. I feel it. The emotions were too strong for it to be otherwise. This girl, I believe with every fiber, was my sister. I press this thought close to my heart and keep it safe there. I won't tell Sam about this.

One thought continues to trouble me long after the memory has gone. It is the only thing that doesn't quite fit. Am I Addison, the missing fourth? If I am Addison, not Abby, why do I have this necklace? Why does Sam call me Abby? Or am I simply wrong about everything, building a fantasy in my head?

CHAPTER THIRTY-THREE

Nine Days Before

I am so alone. Sam is with me but he wants this thing, this happy and lovey, frothy thing that was once me. It used to be so natural, but now I am warped and tangled and wizened and *wrong*, all wrong.

And my head is probably not mine at all because I don't know it. I try to clutch the thoughts that flutter around inside, grab on to them like fireflies and line them up orderly in a glass jar. So I can sort them out, file them, focus. I know I live in my head, and I know Sam says it's bad, that I'm telling myself things that aren't true. But the more I try to go back to how we were, the more uneasy I feel. I don't have any hold on the world around me anymore. I am lost and just drifting.

It's as though someone else lives inside my head. A little gnome, telling me what to think when I want to think something else entirely. Or maybe as if my head is machinery separate from myself. Because my head doesn't know one thing. It knows many, many things; yet I know nothing at all. And so I doubt myself, turn over on myself, and believe nothing.

I was happy in the beginning. It was simple. I basked in it.

I am frightened now.

My fear wedges its hideous face between me and Sam.

I don't know what to do. My brain has become the enemy. Sam is the enemy. I am the enemy. There's no one I can trust, not anyone, not even myself.

CHAPTER THIRTY-FOUR

Nine Days Before

I know it, Sam.

Abby, you're unstable. You're making things up.

I'm not.

You yourself have told me you think something's wrong.

In my head. I laugh. *Something's wrong in my head.*

See? You've made it up. There are a million psychological reasons to support this. He waves around a copy of Jung. He's driving me crazy. He keeps calling me crazy, and it's making me crazy.

Babe, just relax. We can be the way we used to be.

I laugh and laugh and laugh at this.

She's my sister, Sam. I know it. My sister!

Shut UP, Abby!

I lost my sister, Sam. I laugh. Something about this is so funny. Sam wraps his arms around me, and I fight against him for a minute, then I collapse, half crying half laughing, against him.

You're hysterical, he whispers. *Shh, calm down, my baby.* His words are so remote from me. He doesn't understand me at all.

Why are you with me, Sam? Why do you put up with me?

I love you, as complicated and strange as you are.

You really think I am making it all up?

I do, baby. I think you're depressed. You're unhappy with us so you're creating a fantasy in order to escape.

What an awful fantasy, I say. *Couldn't I have come up with something a little better?*

Sam laughs. *You always were the morbid type.*

Was I? Always?

As long as I've ever known you.

How long is that?

Stop asking silly questions. You'll only upset yourself.

I'm so confused, Sam, I say. And I am. I'd thought the evidence linking me to Katherine James, the girl in the photo, was irrefutable. I thought I'd begun to solve the mystery of That Night, of Who I Am. But as it turns out, I can't sift through my thoughts at all. They're a bunch of tangled wires in a knot. Maybe Sam has been right all along. There is some relief in that. I sigh. There would be relief in getting back what we had, in giving up all this detective work.

I just want to be how we were, I say, and in the moment I truly believe it.

Me, too, baby. We can, if you would just let go of it all. Let me take care of you again. Let us be happy.

But Sam, you are sick all the time now. How will you take care of me?

I'll figure it out. I'll take care of everything.

Is it your medicine, Sam? Will it make you better?

Yes, yes, I think so, baby. I need it.

Why won't Sid give it to you?

Don't worry about it. I'll figure it out.

He sounds so confident that I decide to believe him. I relax against him, and as I do, I feel my mind release some of its tension. When I am not fighting against Sam, my mind stops fighting against itself as hard. It is a beautiful serenity. I can tell Sam's being strong for me, and I only feel so guilty that he must. As I watch his face, the way it spasms and the way he sweats, I understand that he is working hard to control his own mind in an attempt to push down the sickness. Sometimes he is sick to his stomach all over the floor. Sometimes he is sick for days at a time. Some times are better than others, like now. But I wonder how long he will be strong. We are both frail creatures right now, and we must support each other. I must take care of him and stop worrying over myself.

I help him over to the couch and settle him there, then busy myself at the stove preparing him some soup. As I stir, the fragrant scent of chicken drifts up and nourishes me, giving me strength and comfort. I feel nearly happy, nearly at ease.

Then I look into the bowl and scream and scream.

Three dead roaches stare up at me with accusing eyes. They bob angrily in tepid water.

I scream until Sam pulls himself from the couch and, with great effort, takes me away from the stove.

Abby, stop, he says in the voice of someone hopeless. *Please, just stop.*

CHAPTER THIRTY-FIVE

Seven Days Before

Where is it, exactly? I ask him. Sam's bent in half on his bed, doubled over from the constant pain he feels all over his entire body. He's worse than usual today.

It's a block west of the high school, he tells me in a weak voice. *Ask for Tom and tell him I sent you. It should take you thirty minutes to get there, thirty minutes to get back. Five minutes there. Be back in an hour, Abby.* His voice carries an edge of warning. It's evidence of Sam's poor state of health that he's willing to send me out at all, after what happened with the library. He hasn't let me out of his sight in what feels like eternity, so it's exhilarating even to think of taking a walk into town, but frightening, too. It means Sam is getting sicker. And part of me is worried that if he keeps getting sicker, one day he'll fade away altogether. I push this from my mind because I know deep down Sam would never abandon me.

I troop down the familiar path through a mile of thick woods. I emerge behind the school. It is the middle of the afternoon. I walk quickly around the side of the large, concrete structure. Through the windows, I can see the outlines of kids hunched over their books in class. I realize that I've been staring when one set of eyes catches my own. There's something familiar in them, but it takes me a second to recognize the blond mop of the boy from the library. His green eyes brighten, and he puts his pencil down, straightening up in his seat. His lips part as if he is about to mouth something to me from the other side of the window. My heart speeds up, and I glance back down, breaking into a quick jog. It won't do to have anyone recognize me; particularly a boy my age. But I know there's no real reason to worry; no one will recognize me here. Sam refuses to tell me how to get to the other town, the one where he saved me that night. To protect me, he says. It can't be far, but the woods are dense, so dense. The wrong direction could lead me deeper, until I'm lost altogether. So I stick to our familiar path.

I can feel the boy's eyes on my back as I run around the edge of the building and away from the school. I will have to take a different route back. If he were to confront me again, start asking questions . . . I shudder at the thought. As Sam's pointed out a million times, no one can know about our woodland kingdom-home. We are too young. We will be sent away if anyone finds out. Sam cleared it out himself, he tells me. He made it a home. It makes me love him more.

When I reach the deli, I am out of breath and nervous because the school's still in sight. I pull open the glass door and try to act like I'm not rushing in. There's an old man, bald, with a thin white mustache, working behind the counter. He eyes me suspiciously.

Why aren't you in school? he asks. *It's still ten minutes till final bell.*

I got an early leave, I mumble, hoping my excuse sounds convincing. Then, as he continues to peer at me closely, *Is Tom here?*

Tom's in back. But the man doesn't budge, doesn't ring a bell, doesn't call for Tom. Nothing.

I just need to ask him something, sir.

Tom! he shouts. *Some girl here to see you!*

A skinny kid a few years older than I am walks out of the back, wiping his hands on a dish towel that's draped from an apron at his waist. He has a goatee and freckles. Before he can say he doesn't know me, I jump in.

Hey, Tom, I say. *Sam says hello.* I watch as Tom's eyes flicker with understanding, and I wonder where Sam knows him from. He motions me to the side, and luckily another customer, a middle-aged woman, walks in just as he does. She looks at me with pursed lips and sniffs quickly before turning toward the old man, who busies himself taking her order. I am relieved for the distraction.

So you're Sam's girl, Tom says, like it's a fact.

Abby, I tell him.

Well, Abby, I'll tell you what. Go wait out back, don't let the old geezer see you, and I'll be out in a minute. I nod and walk back toward the door.

Nice seein' you, Abby! Tom calls loudly in my direction. *Thanks for stopping in.* I wave quickly before shutting the door behind me and heading around back, where the trash cans are. This all seems so strange. I had assumed that all this time Sam was going to the grocery store, bringing back our supper. But now I wonder if he was getting most of our food for free. I never thought much about it before—how we got our food and our furnishings. Everything was just there and perfect and there was no real need to question it. I don't remember feeling hungry at all until now, although I don't remember having had food for days. Did we always have food? It seems that way, but now I'm not sure. I massage my temples; my thoughts are getting cluttered again.

I wait five minutes, then maybe ten, already more than Sam said I should. *Where is Tom?* My eyes automatically dart toward the funny horseshoe-shaped sculpture on the front lawn of the high school. I commune with it for good luck. I watch as the doors to the high school open and kids begin to stream out of its iron gate, and suddenly I'm excruciatingly uncomfortable. They all split up and head in different directions. One little group of four girls is heading toward me. I turn my back to them and lean against the wall, facing the other direction. I am praying they don't notice me. I hear them enter the store and come back out with their food, and still no Tom. Now the girls are sitting on a long picnic bench near me. I can hear them whispering and giggling. I glance at the one girl, a pretty blonde, and see her looking at me the same way the woman in the store did: with her lips curled and her nose turned up. I look away again just as her friends burst into a fit of laughter.

What smells *around here?* says one of the others in an unnaturally loud voice. The blond girl snorts with laughter, and I feel my face heating up.

Seriously, says another, *hold on to your purses, girls.*

My eyes are welling with tears, and I am just about to give up and run home when Tom comes out, finally, with a plastic bag. He hands it to me and sends them a glare.

Thanks for your order, miss, he says to me. I am feeling too anxious and upset to give him more than a grateful nod, then I take off down the street. I'll need to enter the woods from another direction now that people might be watching me. I silently curse Sam for sending me out right at the end of the school day. I turn back just as I'm nearly to the end of the street, and as I do, I notice another figure has joined the girls at the deli. The blond boy is sitting with them, now, talking—but his eyes are trained on mine. He lifts his hand in a small wave. I turn stiffly without returning his wave, run down the street the rest of the way and turn the corner at the end, blocking the scene from view. My heart is thudding rapidly.

I've attracted too much attention; now I've seen this boy enough times for him to recognize me—even wonder about me, if he wanted to. Sam was right; it was so stupid of me to ever go to the library that day.

When I'm safely into the woods, I take a look inside the bag: two enormous sandwiches, stuffed full of ham and turkey, each as long as my arm. Little Styrofoam containers of macaroni and potato salad. My mouth is watering, but I will wait for Sammy. My stomach is so used to being needy that it long ago stopped growling for fuel; but I feel its vengeance now in my faltering limbs. I begin sprinting back the rest of the way, painfully aware of the burning in my chest and the weakness in my legs. When I stop running, it is only because I feel as if I might pass out.

The cave is dim when I enter. The candle next to Sam's bed has burned low, and only the skylight illuminates the room. Sam's fast asleep with one hand draped over the side of the bed. It was silly for me to be nervous; he isn't strong enough to be angry. I shake him gently, and he stirs, rolling over. I gasp. The front of his shirt is caked in dried vomit, and he is so pale.

Sammy?

Eat without me, Abby.

Can I do anything?

No, babe. I just want to sleep.

So I begin to eat, and my food tastes better than

anything I've had in ages. And it doesn't turn into a tenderloin, or a roast pig, or anything more than what it is. But I enjoy it all the same, maybe even more, because I know that my brain is steady. As Sam sleeps, he dreams something horrible; he is awash with nightmares—it's obvious by the way he thrashes and roars in his sleep. But by now, I am used to it. I wrap the other sandwich to save for another day.

CHAPTER THIRTY-SIX

Four Days Before

I have discovered that the roaches were not just in my soup. And I don't think their presence in my soup was a trick of my brain. Now that I have found roaches everywhere— below our mattress, in the plastic bag with our food, under our desk, skittering, lounging, running pell-mell—now I think that maybe the *chicken* was the foreign presence in my soup, mustered up by my fickle brain. I wonder when the last time I even had chicken was. It's a frustrating revelation.

Ever since I registered the presence of the roaches in my life, I have been cleaning. I have been cleaning and clean- ing like a maniac for two days now. Sometimes the walls sparkle; sometimes they're draped in filth. Sometimes I think there is no real reason for me to scrub as I do because everything looks immaculate—better than immaculate: *shining* and *splendorous.* Then other times I see the filth, the rot. And I clean because I figure, better safe.

I have an old broom Sam brought back long ago. I'm not sure where he got it. I use a T-shirt of mine and water from the creek for scrubbing. But it takes buck- ets and buckets; the water turns a filthy black in just minutes, and the T-shirt is useless after a while. I feel as though I'm scrubbing dirt *in* rather than off. So instead I begin to tidy up, bundling up as much garbage as I can into the bag left over from the sandwiches.

When I finish with that, I sort through Sam's and my small collection of shirts, underwear, and jeans. I strip off what I'm wearing and walk to the creek with my arms full of clothing, wearing only a tank top and underwear so I can wash as much as possible right now. Then I dunk everything in and begin to scrub, using nothing but the water.

As I'm washing, it hits me how alone I am, but what's even more startling is that I don't mind being alone. When Sam used to go out to Sid's, or go out for our food, or whatever it was he did with Amanda all the time, my heart would ache. My nerves would be on edge until he returned. It was as if half of me had gone with him and the other half was in pain, missing what it needed to function. But now I am fine, almost peaceful, on my own. And in fact, Sam is at Sid's right now—not in bed, where he's been continuously for the past week.

When Sam pulled himself out of bed around noon or so, he looked no less weak.

I can't stand it any longer, he told me. *I'm getting worse, not better.*

So let me go, I'd said.

No. His reply was firm, almost angry. In it, he sounded strong again. *No. You're never going to that place again. I'll work it out myself.* I was relieved. My last and only trip to Sid's was a big haze that left behind only bad feelings, no tangible memories. But even so, when I look back to it, I feel sick. So now Sam's at Sid's. I feel hopeful, almost happy. All I want is for him to be OK again.

I finish the wash, even doing the sheets, until the trees around our home look like the victims of a bad Halloween prank. Colorful shirts, jeans, sheets — they're draped from every sturdy limb. It's a strange, beautiful sight. I smile at my work. Maybe I will sketch it later so I'll always remember it.

I walk back in, surveying the rest of the room. Our room that once looked cavernous is indeed still cavern-ous but not in size. As I stare, the edges of my vision become blurry and I see one cot and one mattress, each covered in Swiss-cheese holes. One dirty basin, a few tin cups, an upside-down crate, scraps of paper — my sketches — and garbage littering the ground. I close my eyes and open again and try not to focus too closely. I glance quickly at everything, keep my eyes moving, and see two beds, an oak writing desk, a kitchen stove, a sofa, my art framed and hung on the walls. I want it to be that way, so I hang on to it. I don't look too closely. I'm afraid that if I do, I'll see something else, something worse. And that Sam will be right: *I am crazy.* I'm terrified of what it might mean to be crazy.

I walk toward Sam's and my bed. The mattress looks

like it needs a good flip. *A good flip.* There's something in the phrase that feels warm, that conjures up an image of a kind-faced woman struggling with a mattress in a bright, canary-yellow room. She asks for my help; together we flip it.

But here I'm on my own. I put both arms under the unwieldy thing, and I was right: dust billows from its trenches into my nose, nearly suffocating me. Perhaps instead of a flip, it needs a beating, the way women beat rugs with brooms outdoors in some of Sam's books. But I don't think I'm strong enough to carry it outside myself, so a flip will have to do. I've nearly got it up on its side when I hear something slide across the floor and hit the wall. I allow the mattress to fall with a thud on its other side, sending waves of dust up into the air. Coughing, I drop to my knees and feel under the edge of the mattress.

I find an object, small and square and leathery. I pull it out. A notepad. Not just any notepad: *my* notepad. I had forgotten all about it until now. But *why* was Sam keeping it? He told me he would get rid of it, that it was no good. Even stranger, why was it hidden under our mattress?

I collapse to the floor. I am more exhausted than I'd thought, and it's as if this discovery has wiped away any last energy. Just as I've begun to feel safer with Sam, to feel like maybe we are a team again, I find this. I feel all my old doubts and suspicions bubbling to the top of my throat. I feel the old anger, helplessness, frustration.

Why would he do this? What does he want with my old notepad?

Nevertheless, I am glad to have it. It is possibly the one link I have to the girl I used to be. I thumb through its pages carefully, examining the sketches I'd forgotten. I wonder where these images came from, what kind of a girl I was when I drew them.

As I'm absently looking, lost in my imaginings, something slips from the back.

A picture. The class photo kind, posed and rarely valuable to anyone.

But this one, to me, is worth my life.

It is unmistakably, irrefutably, the girl from the newspaper, necklace and all, smiling up at me. My breath catches in my throat. The pain in my forehead bowls me over and fades again just as quickly. Hands trembling, I turn the photo to its back side.

For you, sister-pie. xo, Katie

Katie. Katherine James.

I tear to the back of the notepad, because how could I have missed this before? I flip through the whole thing, quickly, then more quickly, for suddenly all the time in the world has diminished to practically *no time at all,* since I have no idea when Sam will return. Sam. Sam, who knew about this all along. Sam, who knew the truth but tried to convince me I was crazy.

Finally in the back I find it: the little attached

envelope that must have only contained this one photo, because it's empty now. But it doesn't matter; this photo offers me the only proof I need. The girl from my dream, the girl who died in the fire, this girl—they're one and the same. This girl was once someone very close to me, someone Sam wants me to know nothing about. I am Addison, not Abby. I must be. My mind races. The fire, that night—it must be the same. I was there the night Katie James died. I am Addison James.

I clutch my chest. My heart's frantic beats threaten to propel me into a state of panic. As calmly as I can, I place the photo back in the tiny envelope sleeve and put the whole thing back underneath the mattress. Sam won't be able to tell the mattress is flipped. Even to me, it's obvious that the "fresh" side is just as filthy as its opposite. I wiggle the notepad back under, about where it fell, hoping against hope it's in the same approximate spot Sam hid it originally. I only have one option now: to act as though nothing has happened. It will be no easy task if my head continues to spin the way it is.

I busy myself pulling our clothes down from the trees, where they have mostly dried in the sun. If I leave them overnight, they'll be damp with dew in the morning, and it's already beginning to get dark. My mind is awash with the knowledge that now, with what I have discovered, I must leave Sam. But the thought of leaving him while he is ill tortures me with guilt, and the thought of being without him at all is still too difficult to really confront. Maybe he will come back from Sid's with his medicine, and then he will be well, and I won't have to worry about leaving him, and maybe once I find out the truth about that night, I can return to him and he will forgive me for leaving, even understand. My body feels light with hope.

It has been dark for an hour, and I have just started wondering if something bad has happened when Sam drags in. One eye is half-closed, there is blood all over his face, and he is clutching his side as he staggers inside. I shriek and run up to his side just before he collapses altogether. He is racked with silent sobs. I help him move to the bed, but with my every touch, he howls in pain.

Oh, Sam, what happened?

I didn't get it, Abby, he wails in the voice of someone who is tortured. *I didn't get it,* he says over and over. *What will I do? What will I do?*

For a fleeting moment, I wonder if my thoughts of leaving him, my planned betrayal of him, brought this pain upon him, and I feel guiltier than ever before. But I know that can't be. I dab at his face with a T-shirt (I am beginning to run out of them) and am glad to see the blood made him look worse than he really is. He has a black eye and a broken nose, maybe a broken rib. My heart, so vulnerable from its ups and downs of the day, drops once again as I realize that one thing is certain: I will never be able to leave Sam like this.

CHAPTER THIRTY-SEVEN
I have a memory.

We're nestled up in the tree, laughing, Katie and I. Her round little face is beautiful. I adore her, purely and truly.

Hey, *she says,* look, quick! Look out there! *I peer through the branches and see the deer she's pointing to. It pauses, ears alert, its fawn behind it, before scampering off beyond the cemetery, back and back to wherever it came from.*

What do you think's out there? *I ask. The forests seem so vast and frightening, and Mama's always warning us not to wander into them.*

I don't know, *Katie says.* But don't look so scared. It can't be bad, if that little deer lives there.

No, *I agree.* I bet it's magical in the forest.

Of course it is, *says Katie, pressing her cheek against mine, her hot peppermint breath filling the space in front of my nose.* We'll go there someday, when we're older. But for now, this tree is our magic.

And it does look magical. We're concealed by its thick branches, unknown to anyone but the birds that sit above and around us. Even the squirrels don't seem to mind us by now. But then we come here almost every day. It's as if we've become a part of nature.

Katie has a pen out and is pressing its point into the bark of the tree.

Stop! *I cry.* You're hurting it!

I'm not, silly. Don't you want us to be a part of it forever? *I nod slowly, unsure. It looks painful, the way she digs that pen into the bark.*

There, *she says when she's finished,* we'll have to do it again soon, or the bark will heal.

Like skin. This tree, like me, is a living thing. I wonder if maybe we should leave it alone. I don't tell Katie this, because she'll be mad. Instead, I lean my back against hers, where she's perched behind me in the crook of the largest branch, and we stay there, back-to-back for support, until it's time to go home for dinner.

CHAPTER THIRTY-EIGHT

Two Days Before

It hurts, Abby! Sam's voice is urgent, and he shakes my shoulders hard.

Can't you feel it? It hurts! What's happening to me? Now he's itching all over.

He stalks across the room, scratches his ribs until long red streaks cover his chest, bangs his head once, twice on the wall. I am afraid to enter his radius. He's been suffering worse than ever since he came back from Sid's a few days ago without his medicine. It's as if he's begun to give up. He looks like a whirling dervish, a beautiful god-creature with sparks emanating from his mouth. But his violence is too familiar to be glorious.

I see only the beauty. I want to go embrace Sam and lie with him on our canopied bed of purple and green and gold, but I know it isn't safe. The other world — the one we hate, the one we call Circle Nine — is breaking through Sam's protective armor and turning him into someone else.

That is why, even though I feel light and safe right now, I know I must offer. I look at him, and he meets my eyes, and I know he is thinking the same.

What can I do? I ask it quietly.

He pauses. Then, through gritted teeth and streaming eyes: *You could go back there. You could go back to Sid's. Like we did before.* His head jerks back and forth as though he's shaking the words off, a dog in the rain, even as he says them.

A cold feeling grips me, followed by a wave of heated revulsion so strong it makes me blind. I would do almost anything to help Sam. I thought I could do this. But when I think of that night at Sid's, think of actually going back there, my body turns off completely. It refuses to work. It refuses to obey my mind. As long as I consider going back to Sid's, my body will stay rooted to this spot. My body and Sid are opposing magnetic forces. Sid repels me.

I can't go, I tell him. *I'm sorry.* I am miserable. The words are knives hurtling from my tongue.

Please, he whispers. Tears roll down his cheeks.

Sam, I say, *I just can't do it; I'm sorry.* I am hurting for him, so sorry to deny him anything.

Sam is silent. He turns away, begins sobbing quietly.

Then I am filled with relief; my hot-and-cold panic subsides. I realize: I can go to Sid's, after all. I can find another way, make a different trade.

I'll try, Sam, I tell him suddenly. *I'll go to Sid's and I'll try.* At this, he turns back to me, his eyes alight with watery red hope.

I knew you would, baby. I knew you wouldn't make me suffer.

So I have decided to do the one thing I can to ensure Sam's safety once I am gone. I put my plan into action, gathering supplies, brainstorming a trade that Sid will not refuse. If I don't come back with Sam's medicine, if I don't know for sure that he will be OK, I will not be able to leave. And that is not an option. To stay here will destroy me, too.

When I see Sam's ugliness—his tortured body and venomous words, the things I used to associate only with Circle Nine—I know I am more a part of that world than this one. I know that my time here is over, and it makes me less afraid. The ugliness I see sometimes makes our canopy bed look like a dirty, stained mattress. It makes our feasts of lamb and roasted pears look like McDonald's we pulled from a garbage bin. It does evil, horrible things with what we have and to Sam. Sometimes he turns from me and talks to Amanda's shrine, where it sits in the corner of the room. He talks to the shrine as if it is Amanda herself. Amanda is a good listener, he says. She listens patiently, he says. He says he likes how she does not interrupt like I do. She's easy. She doesn't drive him out of his mind. She sits quietly among her possessions.

I know that Amanda is gone. But even still, I have that old worry that Sam loves Amanda more than he loves me. It is all madness.

Sam, I think, I will go get your medicine, and you'll be OK, and then I can leave you, only for a while, only to do what I need to do.

I think these things, but really I am worried that he will not be able to survive this. I am panicked. I will be able to survive, because now I know that Circle Nine is the world in which I belong. It is where I came from — I know that deep down, from everything I've discovered. But Sam may not be equipped to get on without me here. I hope that his medicine will make him feel better, like before, when I first came here with him. But I also know that his magic-potion medicine isn't safe. I'm suspicious of its cylindrical vial, but I see no other choice.

I leave Sam, thrashing and muttering, behind me, and I plunge into the outdoors. I am less and less vulnerable out here, since now I've left many times on my own. It makes me feel strong, empowered. Besides, when everything is still beautiful and the darkness hasn't crept in, I am invincible.

I trudge over the train tracks, three blocks west to where Sid lives. I have brought Sid a modest gift. I hope it will be enough; it was the best I could do. What happened last time left me feeling dirty, cast me into a bad place. So this has to be enough. It's my only plan. I'm not sure it's a good one, though; something feels off, fills me with a desperate panic.

Sid! I call.

I knock four times. His little house looks so warm and inviting. There are flowers blooming around his white picket fence. There is light streaming from his windows.

Marmalade, Sid's cat, slinks sultry around the corner and rubs against my ankles. She is hairless and adorable. Sid is a true animal lover, Sam told me once. I stroke her chin and she meows and vibrates under my palm. Sid sees me through the window.

What do you want, Abby? He asks it past the door, while it is still shut. *Back for more?*

But he seems afraid of me.

Please, I say. I stand for a few minutes patiently.

Sid finally opens the door a crack. He looks at me and makes a face like he doesn't like what he sees.

Go away, Abby.

He shuts it again. But I push the door open and offer him my fists. My offering is hidden inside my right fist. It is very important that he picks the right fist.

Pick one, I say.

You're crazy.

Pick one, Sid.

I motion my fists at him again. Marmalade yowls at my feet. She wants me to keep petting her. I nudge her with my toe, hoping it will suffice.

Sid rolls his eyes and points to my right fist. I laugh! I am doubled over with mirth. I knew he would choose that one. I am so excited to give Sid what he picked. It means maybe I will get Sam's medicine today, after all. I unroll my fingers from where they clutch at my palm. Inside my fist is my offering. I hold it up. Something's wrong with it.

Sid yells and jumps back. Then he slams the door again.

Freaking crazy, he mutters through the door. *Get the hell out of here and don't come back,* he says. *Freak!*

I don't know at first why he reacted like that. His rudeness settles into my gut and makes me sick. It is a crushing disappointment. Maybe Marmalade will like my offering. I kneel down, and she is already nudging her nose against my fist, which I have closed again. I open it slowly and, as she pounces on the tiny dead mouse, I begin to understand. It wasn't dead this morning; I have clutched it too hard in my sweaty fists. It was sweet and companionable when I caught it—an offering fit for Sid. But now it looks slightly nasty and only fit for a cat. I wipe my palm on my thigh and take a breath. I am angry, but only with myself; my instincts have betrayed me. I need to go back to Sam.

When I return to the cave and Sam sees I am empty-handed, he cries.

I'm sorry, Sammy, I whisper for the millionth time as the tears roll down his cheeks. Without Sam's medicine I am trapped. I curl up behind him on our bed, which has turned into the ugly torn cot again. I wrap my body behind his so all of our parts match up. I kiss the back of his neck as he sobs, and eventually we begin to fall asleep. I have let myself down, too.

CHAPTER THIRTY-NINE
That Night

I am so frightened. I've never seen Sam like this, worse than ever before. He is raging, throwing things, tearing at his hair, and I am sitting quietly in the corner, hoping he won't focus his rage on me. The source of his fury is his medicine, of course—the stuff I used to think of as medicine, but now I know it for what it always was: poison, drugs. The barrier between Circle Nine and my and Sam's world has been broken. Circle Nine is seeping in and swishing around us until nothing's separate any longer. But every now and then there are glimmers of the old brightness. And when there are, I hang on to them, because the alternative threatens to destroy me.

I look at Sam as if he's on a screen and I'm at the cinema, like on our Date not so long ago. With him on the screen, I don't worry for myself. I am free to stare long at the purple marks on his arms, his bony rib cage, and the thinness of his hair. I am free to feel horrified without fear. I look at my own body and see that it's as bony as his, but my arms are free from any marking. There is that. I am so hungry. There is nothing to cook here. There is not even any way of cooking. It's cold, and damp, and filthy, and my Sam is raging, so loud and violent now that I can't keep him on that cinema screen.

He's shaking my shoulders. My teeth rattle against each other, and my neck snaps back.

Why didn't you help me! He is so angry. He slaps me hard, and I am crying. He's never before touched me in this angry way.

I tried, Sammy. I tried so hard.

Why don't you care that I'm suffering, Abby? Why don't you care?

I do care! I plead with him. He is squeezing me too tight and slapping me again and again. I feel trails of tears and maybe blood on my cheeks.

Then do something, Abby, help me! I need it. Don't you see I need it?

I see, Sammy. I see that, I tell him. I don't know what to do.

Now he's crying, too, and saying he's sorry, but he's so different from the Sammy I love that it's hard for me to look at him and know he is the same. I wonder if he has always been like this, but I don't think that could be. As angry as I am with him for what he's done, the things he's hidden, I still can't believe it was all a game for him.

Then he's running outside and I'm running after him, but we're both slow and clumsy. It rained earlier, whole sheets of it slicing the sky in half, and now the ground is soggy. Its damp softness feels like quicksand under my feet. It's late at night, and I'm afraid Sam will get lost or hurt himself, because he's so weak. And I'm afraid I'll lose sight of him. I'm weak, too, but I'm still stronger than he is—strong enough to want to take care of him.

The only thing that fuels him is desperation. I can hear the crunch of his shoes against the ground, and I know he's heading toward town. But I don't know what he plans to do there. He's still crying, and his breath is coming out in thick, animal-like grunts. It is later than late. It is the darkest, deepest part of night now.

We reach town and it's dead. Sam stops for breath, and I try to wrap my arms around him, to calm him, but he shoves me away in one motion far more violent than he should be able to manage. All I can do is follow. My heart pounds because some part of me feels like this is it: every bad and good thing we've ever done in our lifetimes has come down to this moment.

Sam has reached a small liquor store, Canyon Jack's. I am ten paces behind him, lagging, but I can't move faster. My limbs are deadweight, and my head is light and hazy. He stares at the store for a moment, then he walks to the garbage bin that sits outside and rummages around inside. I am afraid to ask questions. My cheek still throbs from earlier, and my left hand is painfully swollen from where I caught myself when he shoved me down. I watch the scene from a distance, watch it unfurl out of my control.

Finally he finds what he is looking for. A large stone meant to weigh down the flimsy plastic bin. Sam launches the stone through the store window. The sound of shattering glass may as well be a bomb going off in this quiet neighborhood, and I wonder if he triggered an alarm. I run up to the window and look in. Sam's already at the cash register. I know what comes next.

Sammy, please, I plead with him. *Please come home with me.*

Just a little, he cries. *Just a little bit, Abby. I'll pay it back—I promise. Just enough for Sid. Please, Abby. I can't do it anymore.* He is sobbing, pathetic, and stuffing wads of cash in his pockets, and again I feel like this isn't real, and I don't know what's real anymore, whether this is Circle Nine or my life or one of my gruesome nightmares. I am so terribly sad.

Just hurry, Sammy! I say, because now I can hear sirens not far away, and they remind me of how scared I was when he saved me from the burned-down house that awful day long ago.

I'm hurrying, baby. Don't leave me.

Hurry!

Now he's leaping over the counter and racing toward me where I stand on the other side of the broken window. But it's going to be too late—I know it is! Because I can see the flickering lights of the police cars reflecting off the buildings down the street. I want to run, but I don't;

I am motionless, waiting for Sam. He is coming toward me fast. He is looking into my eyes as he runs, and they are full of everything that's ever happened to us, and I see how much he loves me and how sad he is. Now he's jumping back through the window because I know he's thinking, No time to unlock the door. I am screaming for him, and I've already begun to back up because he'll be right behind me. When I turn around again, he's not there. I see him rolling on the ground holding his leg and screaming, and there's a puddle of blood trailing from him and blood on the glass above him where he leaped.

Don't leave me, baby! He is crying and gasping it over and over. He is so like a child, lying helpless and hurt, and for a moment I am frozen, caught again in his eyes, in their beautiful brown-gold agony. My eyes dart toward the cars, which are turning the corner with their red and blue lights. Then again at him, at his mouth which even now forms my name. I look at him long, one more time, maybe for the last time, before I turn and run.

I save myself.

PART TWO
WAKING

CHAPTER FORTY

That Night

Maybe he's been caught by now. Maybe he's sitting in some hospital, or a jail cell, afraid. I wonder, I worry, but I don't turn back. It would be impossible. The cave is not far—I remember that much. I move quickly, fighting the irrational fear that he is following behind me. I go fast, faster still until I am stumbling, until I have run for a very long time. Far too long. The dense forest stretches as far as I can see, so far it implies no end. There's silence apart from my breathing, heavy and fast, the rustling of the wind against the trees, the calls of owls or maybe bats. White noise.

Then I know: there is no cave for me anymore, no safe place. It is nowhere; it's been swallowed up by the forest. I'll never find it.

I keep running. It doesn't matter. All that matters is the pain crushing my head and the weary feeling that's oozing up my ankles and toward my shins and over my lungs and chest, making it impossible for me to breathe. I stop, collapse, rest. Right now, I don't know what else to do.

CHAPTER FORTY-ONE

I remember the truth.

For the first time, I see it as it happened.

Mama's curled up next to Daddy on the bed. She keeps to his schedule, usually; so nothing could really wake them between nine p.m. and five a.m., when he gets up for work. When everyone else is up watching movies late at night, they're snoring a duet. When other people get up for breakfast, Daddy's practically taking a lunch break. That's the way it is with him — odd jobs take odd hours. As for Katie, she's gone out again after cheer camp.

It's the perfect time.

I met a boy this morning, Sam. My heart thuds even as I think of him. I have such a hard time meeting people, boys and girls alike; Katie's the more social one, and I've never needed any friends but her. Lately, though, she's been getting impatient with me. "You're sixteen, Addie. Time to start living your own life." So she goes out without me, and I'm left alone a lot of the time with only Mama to talk to. Mama tells me things will change, that I'm just a late bloomer like she was, that Katie got Daddy's natural charm. Mama says it's hard for me to connect, that kids are hard, that I'll find my kindred spirits eventually, that people just need to grow up. Thinking I might bloom later doesn't stop me from being angry with Katie now when she leaves and it's just me.

It's true that Katie and Dad are a lot alike. No matter how tired he is, he always smiles when he sees her, makes a few jokes just to get her grinning, perks up when she walks in the room. When they laugh together, it's like twin wind chimes knocking against each other, musical and airy. Their eyes crinkle up the same way, and they don't stop until they're clutching their stomachs because it hurts. It's different with me. When Daddy looks at me, he looks tired, like maybe it's too much effort to try to make me laugh, too. Like I'm somebody unfathomable, like I don't really belong to him at all.

Today, I met my own friend, someone who doesn't even know who Katie is. To Sam, I am not Katie's little sister. I'm just me, a girl he met. I skipped summer school this morning. I don't do much there, anyway—just sit in the back of the room and daydream and sketch until the final bell rings. I've always kept to myself; no one bothers about me much anymore. I know people think I'm weird, or at best standoffish, but really it just fits to be alone. I used to try; I used to force a smile onto my face and laughter into my voice, even when I didn't get the jokes or the secret teenage language everyone else around me seemed to share. Finally, I realized that all my trying wasn't fooling anyone. So I stopped altogether and drifted back a little. And I liked it fine that way, really.

Today I told Mama I was sick, then slipped out when she was gone running errands. After she got back, she probably jumped right into bustling around the house, getting dinner ready for Daddy, like always. He gets home around four, and after that they usually don't notice a thing but one another, as long as we're back for dinner. It's funny about Mama; she's one-hundred percent devoted to Katie and me, but then when Daddy's around, love takes over and she forgets to focus as hard on us. I think they must be really in love. When they're around each other, they act all young and giddy again. It's OK, though. They're good to us, my parents.

I was on the swing set in the park when I met him. It's where I like to go to think. I was twirling on the swing, doing my thinking, even talking to myself a little when he spoke.

"I talk to myself, too," he said. "I always thought I was crazy till now." I jumped, because I hadn't heard him come up at all, let alone settle onto the swing exactly next to me. I was so embarrassed. The boy was dark and strikingly handsome, Latino-looking. I was pierced, gone from the start.

"I wasn't talking to myself," I muttered, looking at the ground.

"OK," he said. "Then I guess you were talking to me." I looked up then, meeting his eyes and nodding slowly. He looked long and hard at my notepad, open on my lap. It was just a little piece of nothing, a drawing of me, how I see myself. But his eyes went wider when he saw it, and he nodded as if he saw exactly what it was I was doing. As if he saw the thoughts behind the girl in the picture.

"Do one of me?" he asked. So I did, forgetting the way I usually try to normalize things, forgetting to try to flirt the way Katie does, forgetting to focus on anything but the way I saw him in that moment. When I was done, he looked at it for a long time.

"I think I understand," he finally told me after I'd sat there biting my lip for a couple of minutes. His voice was quiet and serious, and I worried at first that I'd offended him. Maybe he hated what I saw. Because what I'd seen was a mishmash of contradictions—some lovely, some harsh—and what I'd drawn was a caricature of that. My interpretation. He wore a shirt with rolled cuffs, once white and probably crisp but now irreversibly soiled, as if he'd been living in it for weeks. It had some embroidery, Rockville Prep, on its breast pocket. I knew Rockville Prep. It was a boarding school an hour away, the kind of place even the rich can barely afford. He wore chinos that were ragged and thin, leather dress shoes with holes in them. His face was hard-edged and handsome, but his eyes were sunken deep. He oozed of ruined wealth. He looked like he'd fallen from grace, so that's what I'd drawn: a fallen angel.

I held my breath, waiting for him to turn angry eyes my way. I shouldn't have done it; I shouldn't have drawn the truth. But then he tore the picture out and put it in his pocket.

"Hope you don't mind," he said.

"I do mind," I told him. "It's mine. Maybe once I get to

know you better, you can have it." I was shocked by my boldness, but he didn't seem bothered.

"Fair enough," he said, handing it back. Then, after another minute, "Icarus. Icarus might have been better. For the drawing, I mean. Better than a fallen angel."

"Daddy always told me any man who describes himself as Icarus has a terrible ego," I said to him. There was another pause, then he surprised me by laughing long and hard.

"Your dad's probably right," he told me.

After that, we talked. We talked for hours and hours, all through the morning and into the afternoon. He told me he wanted to go to Thailand to live in a hut on the beach and read books all day in a hammock and live on nothing but fish he caught himself. I said that sounded nice, that I would come too and peddle my art to tourists on the side of the road. That I'd roast bananas for dessert. That I'd weave mosquito netting for the windows. That I'd let the salt coat my hair until I looked wild and fierce.

He laughed and said, "We're a little different but exactly the same, you know." And then he told me in words heated and passionate about the books he loved the most, and as he talked, I illustrated what I saw in his words, the emotions of it and feelings of it, until my notepad was nearly full. Then I looked at my watch and it was almost time for dinner, and I was sure even my oblivious parents would know I wasn't sick, after all, that I'd just skipped out. I was shocked that *six-and-a-half hours had gone by. I'd never talked that much to any single person in my life, even Katie.*

He was intoxicating, he was brilliant, he opened my mind and heart. He was a dreamer, like me.

"I've got to go," I told him.

"OK," he said. "But I'll miss you." He smiled, wide and crooked, and my heart stopped. I'd barely walked four steps, four heavy steps, when he spoke up again.

"Hey, I hate to ask you this, but . . ." At that point I would have done anything in the world he'd asked for. He looked down, as if he was embarrassed. "I'm just short a few bucks," he said. "Do you have anything? A loan, I mean." My heart plummeted. Money was the one thing I couldn't give him. But then I'd remembered the small safe in Mama and Daddy's room. The way they opened it only on our birthdays or other special occasions. Family money. The money they'd saved up. I nodded slowly. I told him what to do, when to meet me.

So here I am, eleven p.m., staring at Mama and Daddy's sleeping bodies. They look so peaceful next to each other, as if they were born curled up like this. I imagine Sam and me doing the same thing, and I shudder. This afternoon was too wonderful for me to bear. I turn from them and tiptoe back to my room, careful to leave their door open a crack for easier access later. I think how jealous Katie will be when she meets Sam. Or maybe she'll be happy for me, proud of me for finding him and attracting him all on my own. I suddenly can't wait to tell her all about him; I imagine us whispering and giggling like old times.

I stand there daydreaming for another few minutes before I hear it: the slight pinging on my windowpane. I laugh; the pebbles had been his idea. "I've always wanted to," he'd said. I wave to him before running as quietly as I can down the stairs. My heart is thudding. I am betraying Mama and Daddy. But it's just a loan; he said he'd replace it by next week. They only go in that safe every few months, anyway. They'll never even know it was gone. And I trust him, I do.

I let Sam in the front door, and we tiptoe upstairs together. What we're about to do is wrong and I know it, but I am high, so very high on adrenaline and giddiness and the inexplicable, incomparable attraction I feel for him. He clutches my hand and places one finger to his lips, and then I'm fighting giggles; it's one big adventure. This whole day has been. The fun of it makes what we're actually doing easier to ignore.

When we reach my parents' door, I push it open ever so carefully. It emits a small creak, but it's not loud enough to wake them. Just to make sure, I hold my breath and wait another thirty seconds, counting it out—"one, one thousand," like that—in my head. Then we creep in soundlessly. The room smells like cookies baking, and my eyes are immediately drawn to the flickering candles on their windowsill. Mama's doing. She's forgotten, as usual, to put them out, but now *their light leads us, an accomplice to our crime. The smell is suffocating as I inch my way toward the small safe Daddy had installed into the wall right next to their bed. The room itself is dingy and gray and littered with scraps of paper and candy wrappers, Mama's hair spray and bottles of nail polish in every color. In the corner is Daddy's model-plane set, bits of balsa wood littering the floor below a cheap folding table. Neither of my parents is tidy. There's a thin sheet covering the only window in lieu of a curtain, blocking out prying eyes. I don't know the code to the safe, but Sam told me he knows how to use a bobby pin, and the code itself is way too loud to use even if I did know it.*

I'm waiting behind Sam and he's fumbling with the pin and my armpits are feeling damp and Mama seems more restless than usual, grunting a little and drooling, although maybe this is what she always does. I've never seen it up close. They've been out for nearly two hours, plenty long enough, I estimate, for them to be in REM. But who knows whether they are or not? Long enough is no guarantee, and two of them means double the chance we'll be caught. The desperation of my plan washes over me in full, but Sam's in it both hands now, jiggling that bobby pin for all it's worth, and the way he seems so assured of everything calms me down a little.

Then there's a click. Silence.

The door swings wide and, thank God, they haven't spent all of it or even close to it, and I help Sam grab it, jamming bill after bill into my pockets and down my shirt into my bra.

I'm so excited, I don't feel Sam's hand on my wrist, pulling me away, pointing at my mama, who's rolling over, as if she's about to wake up. But something about the situation has taken hold of me, and it's as if my hands won't stop reaching into that safe.

I pull away and feel my skin begin to slide through his wrist, and then I am free, except momentum makes my arm jerk back and it collides with something, and that same something falls from the sill, hitting my arm and leaking searing, hot wetness over me. I smell cookies baking on my wrist.

There is a wave of intense heat. It pushes me backward into Sam. Something's gone wrong.

Now the place is on fire. Everything is ablaze. I stare at it, wondering how it could have happened so quickly. Then Mama is awake, rubbing her eyes in confusion, mumbling incoherently. I look at Sam and wonder why he is still standing there, why he isn't running away, and then I realize that he's stamping at the flames frantically, but then they're spreading and his stamping's doing no good, and the smoke is so thick I can barely see, and we're both hacking madly, and he's pleading with me to come with him. The flames have spread between me and Mama and Daddy.

I am suddenly more afraid than I have ever been in my life. I fight Sam and turn to go back, but his grip is iron. He is strong, much stronger than I am. Now we're at the door, and I give in, allowing him to pull me closer to it, farther from my parents. I find the doorknob first with my hands, but when I try to turn it, it melts my fingers and wrist on impact, and I scream. I watch as Sam pulls his shirt off and uses it as a glove, and then the door is wide open and we are gloriously free, since the smoke isn't as bad in this part of the hall.

But Mama and Daddy are not behind us. I turn back for them one more time, but I can't see them. I can't even tell anymore which direction I am pointed, because I am so disoriented by the flames. All this time, Sam's hand never leaves my wrist. The flames are miles high already and block the stairs to the attic, but the stairs to the main level are still intact and that's where he pulls me. I mutter prayers under my breath that Mama and Daddy will be OK. Maybe they have already jumped from their second-story window.

Sam pushes me to the ground and we start down on all fours, me in front and him behind. And when I wake up, there is an angel above me, stroking my cheek, and I can't remember a thing.

CHAPTER FORTY-TWO
That Night

I don't want the memories. I struggle to my feet; I run from him and I run from them. I run from Abby, too, that person I was and wasn't, the person Sam wanted me to be. I run fast at first and then never fast enough, tree branches whipping my face and midnight sounds hissing just behind my heels. I move like this, on and on and on—a crazed automaton—until I am reduced to nothing but blood and sweat and tears. Will I die like this out here? I run for what must be hours. I've run the wrong way; I've known it all along, but I also don't know which is the right way. I expected to see the big rock, the faded trampled-out path, fresh from our feet. Then the pond, lovely and shining under the moon, and the cave not far behind it.

But all I've seen for miles are trees, thick trees with rocks and brambles scattered in between. My pants are torn. There is mud everywhere; it saturates me until I feel I am made of clay. I have no direction, only forward. There's only one thing I feel profoundly: exhaustion. I want to sleep; I must sleep or I will die. I must keep moving or I will die. I take one more step and hope that with it will come something new: a road, or water—because I am horribly, painfully thirsty, so thirsty I am dizzy—or maybe some sign of human life. But there's nothing; and maybe it wouldn't be so bad, I think at last, to sleep, just for a little while.

CHAPTER FORTY-THREE

One Day After, Eleven a.m.

I open my eyes as I do every other day, but today there's the brightness of sun in my face. It's unusual; there's usually no sunlight in the cave. We have to go outside for our sun. "Sam?" I ask. "Sammy?" He doesn't answer me. I roll over, and there's something sharp and prickly in my face. My face. My face is on fire. I reach up and scratch it and claw at it because it feels like I've got some horrible itching disease, and I call for Sammy but he doesn't come, and I open my eyes and—

I am not in the cave at all. Not at all. I am somewhere vast and, even though it has all the same things: trees and brambles and bugs and animal noises and dirt— none of it's familiar. I claw at my face and remember. He's gone. I left him. I scratch harder and snarl, the way I imagine an animal might, because that's what I'm feeling: animal pain. Animal pain and otherpain, pain inside. I look down, and my fingernails are bloody. It feels good. It distracts from the otherpain.

It was my fault.

I sit up; a wave of dizziness and nausea overcomes me. I vomit up nothing onto the ground. I scratch more, then I scratch the hands I'm scratching with. My arms are covered in ugly red welts that have made them swollen and inflamed as if there's a nest of mosquitoes living right there under the skin. I touch my face again. It's probably the same, but I don't care. I am empty and exhausted; most of me just wants to lie back down.

My fault.

But then there's this other part of me. *Move, move, move,* it says. *You won't die here like this. You can't.*

I laugh and laugh and laugh because I am *so stupid* and that voice is wrong because I *can* die out here and maybe I even want to. I laugh as I'm on my knees, crawling, as I'm standing up, taking steps I didn't know I could, as I'm moving forward, and the worst part is I don't know where I'm moving forward *to;* maybe I'm moving even farther away from where I should be moving, and this realization is even more hilarious. I laugh and walk, walk and laugh, choke on my own laughter, stumble on swollen legs, look around me at all these things I never noticed before that seem surreal, maybe enchanted. I am so thirsty.

Maybe I'm in an enchanted forest and if I just fall asleep, a prince will wake me up. Maybe the prince will be Sam; he'll be well again and nothing will be wrong with him, and he'll run one palm across my cheek and my whole face will heal up just like magic, and everything will be OK. Everything will be OK. Even if I die, everything will be OK.

I don't know time anymore; in this place, time doesn't

exist, anyway. It's just more of the same. Trees and rocks and bugs and dirt. Trees and rocks and bugs and dirt. I say this through my lips, which have turned to wood, firewood. I laugh some more. If a tree falls and you don't hear it, does it really fall? If a girl dies in the woods and you don't find her, is she really dead? Was she ever alive?

It's hot in the shade. I need a gas station to pump some fuel into me or my engine will stall. It's about to stall. It does. There's no fuel for my legs, so they give out first and I'm back to the earth, where I was before, where I came from in the first place.

I'm just so exhausted. It occurs to me that I really could die here, that I am too tired to go on, and that maybe I will lie here until I am too thirsty or too hungry to live, whichever comes first. Until my body betrays me. And if that happens, it wouldn't be so bad; my story will die with me. No one will ever know the truth. I am filled with relief at this thought. *There will be nothing to tell.*

When the memory washes over my tired soul, it's vivid and powerful. I surrender to it because I can't find the strength not to.

Mama is awake. The flames have spread between me and Mama and Daddy. Mama screams, but I am transfixed. I watch her makeshift curtains light up magically. It's a beautiful light show before me, and even my parents look beautiful, for by now their sheets are on fire and they appear ethereal. But there is something wrong here; I feel the frantic desire to leave. Something is terribly wrong. The fire is spreading fast, as if the house was glued together with lighter fluid. I'm finding it hard to breathe and now to see, and Sam's grip on my wrist grows tighter, and this time I allow him to lead me through the haze across the room, even though I hear Mama and now Daddy screaming my name.

I see my mother's face and I am cold. I see my mother's face and horror turns me to ice. I am in the core of Circle Nine, the world I loathed and feared. I am shivering, sickened, destroyed. All I want, I think, is to have my family back. All I want is to be forgiven. But still, one voice in my head won't let me go.

What about Katie? the voice asks. *What happened to her?*

I don't know, I say back. I'm sorry. I'm so, so sorry.

Yet the voice stays with me. I can't give up, not yet, not while I don't know everything. I force myself to stumble on.

CHAPTER FORTY-FOUR

The Evening After, Five p.m.

Gunshots.

I am tired, so tired. It is hard to know what's going on.

An epic war is going on around me; I wonder if I've been hit.

Boom. Screaming. A furry thing tears by me. It's crying blood.

Yet I keep walking.

A pair of brown boots in front of me.

Voices, voices all around. I hover in the voices.

"Are you OK? Miss, are you OK?"

I nod. A hand on my shoulder brings me back, just a little.

"Are you hurt?" A long look at my face. "Did someone hurt you?"

"No," I whisper. A look of doubt.

More voices: "She looks terrible." . . . "Shhhh."

"Where do you live?"

"Here." I gesture. "Right here. I've been out here for a while," I hear myself say in a dreamy voice. I'm awfully tired.

"Come on. We'll get you some help." A gentle hand, and I'm being lifted, carried, placed in a truck. I don't mind. I'm tired, so tired.

Darkness.

CHAPTER FORTY-FIVE

The Evening After, Seven p.m.

The voices fade in and out. They swirl around me, lifting me up on a cloud of comfort. I am buoyant. They are angels.

"She's doing fine. Just a little dehydrated, and exhausted, I'd say."

"She looks like she could sleep for days."

"Maybe she will."

"Nothing serious, then?"

"Could've been much worse. Nearly had a heart attack when I seen her."

And there's a little angel, too.

"Will she be OK? Will she, Dad?"

As I dream, I feel promise filling my body; I become limp and light and entirely free from pain, as if I've been lifted out of my shell and taken somewhere better. I feel close to everything I ever lost and wanted back. My mother, my father, and Katie. And Sam. Sam, whole and beautiful again, the way he was when he stood over me that day long ago, eyes so innocent and longing and strong and full of promise. I'm warm all over, and there's something else I feel, something foreign and wonderful. I'm at peace. I want it. I want to stop struggling. I want this peace.

CHAPTER FORTY-SIX

Two Days After

"Hasn't seen a decent meal in weeks, by the look of it. She's so scrawny."

"Thank God you found her. Who knows what she was doing out there all alone. And that bruise on her face! Could've been much worse."

I can open my eyes. I can see the room around me. There's a man in camouflage and hunting boots staring at me, arms crossed. There's a woman holding a mug. I'm on a cot. The springs of it dig into my back. The room is small; the walls close in on me. I close my eyes again; I don't want this. I wanted to die.

"No way, kiddo," says the woman. "You've been out for a full day. Now that you're back with us, you're staying. Don't get any big ideas." Her face looms, kind and round, above me. "Just to give you your strength," she tells me, handing me the mug, which has a seductive-smelling broth in it. "Just some fluids."

I sip it slowly, savoring its warmth; then I close my eyes and will these people away, pretending to sink back into sleep for just a little while longer.

They leave me in peace, and I let my mind drift. I can't

help but turn to my memories. Now I know what happened in the fire. *My fault. All my fault.*

But what about Katie?

The pain in my head is tremendous.

CHAPTER FORTY-SEVEN

I Remember Katie.

I remember her now. Her black hair would become matted and snarled when she slept, so bad that she used to spend what seemed like hours each morning combing it out before our mother came to wake us. Her bed was above mine, and sometimes the stray strands drifted down around me in the space between our beds, and I imagined they formed a protective orb around the rusted frames. I remember the way she meticulously cut her bangs, always a little too short, one metal blade pressed against her forehead as she watched herself in the mirror, fringe falling softly to the sink. I remember the way she kicked at the sink when nothing but a rusted trickle came from it instead of real water and Daddy hadn't fixed it because he was too tired from pulling a double shift. Fire. And how she lived: wild and defiant and barely muted at all, despite everything. I remember her name. Katie. I whisper it over and over, hoping it will feel familiar, then again when it doesn't. I sink back into memories of her laughing, her twirling my hair around one index finger, her pressing her bony cheek against mine when things were bad, whistling at the boys across the street through the slats of the attic shutters where we couldn't be heard by Mama. She was the greatest source of joy I ever knew. We were supposed to be invisible when debt collectors came to the door. We were invisible anyway, the way you are when you're a gangly teenager and you can't afford nice things to wear—you can't afford anything, really, because you live in a house but also on the streets, both places equally your home. Then Sam made us disappear altogether. Even before then, the world wasn't my own.

I close my eyes, and her voice fills my head.

You see? it whispers. *I've been trying to tell you all along.*

I know, I whisper back. *But I couldn't listen to you just yet.*

I think of the day she gave me the necklace.

"Ghetto-fab-o-lous," she says, drawling the word as she slips the chain over my neck.

"You've got to be kidding me." The necklace spells Abby *in gold loopy script, bling-bling style, with a tiny diamond at the bottom of the* y. *"Um," I say, "this isn't my name?"*

"Let's just say there weren't that many available," she replies. Then it dawns on me.

"Katie! Did you steal *these?" She smiles wickedly and wiggles her eyebrows up and down at me. I am horrified and delighted. I could never be like Katie is. She is larger than life, without even trying to be.*

"Oh, come on, Addie-cakes. Stop being such a bore. It's the closest thing to Addie *that they had,* OK? *At least that I could grab. Plus, it's kinda cute. Maybe I'll start calling you*

Abby forever." She gives me a wink. "And I know you've got an inner thug somewhere in there, Miss Addison. Do me a big ol' favor and embrace it for once!"

Katie's doubled over laughing. She knows I'm about the least thuggy person in the history of this world. But I love my necklace anyway.

"Now, hide it," she says, and I tuck it under my sweatshirt, confused.

"Katie . . ." I start.

"Shhh." She puts one finger over her lips.

"But where did you—?"

"SHHH!" she practically shouts, looking at me mock sternly. "Not another word, all right?" She flashes her own necklace, identical to mine except for the name, Katie*—at least she got hers right—before tucking it back under her own long-sleeved T-shirt.*

"Now, get back inside," she says to me. "And don't show Mama. Our little secret."

"Where are you going?" I ask as she begins to turn and walk back out the gate that marks the entrance to our front yard.

"Never mind that, Abby," she says. "Quit being such a tagalong."

At that, I feel a quick burst of something like anger, but just as quickly, it's gone. And then I can't help it. I run after her and tackle her in a huge hug, and before I know it, she's elbowing me off her scrawny self and squirming away and we're lying next to each other on the grass for all the world to see, dying laughing, just happy.

I remember so much now. But not the way she died; I can't remember that. I reach back, and there's only guilt and pain.

CHAPTER FORTY-EIGHT

Three Days After

I'm propped up on the cot, a warm green fuzzy blanket tucked around my legs, my body drowning in an unfamiliar oversize T-shirt. The blanket is the kind maybe somebody's mother would make. It hits me: it's the kind my mother used to make. The knowledge is enough to make me taste bile. I turn to the side and dry-heave toward the bag on the ground next to me. I am immediately glad I didn't vomit, because in the bag is what remains of my filthy clothing, along with the *Inferno*, Sam's tattered book. I shouldn't be surprised that it's here — I've always kept it close — but somehow I am. In this warm, sterile room, it seems like a relic from another world. I'm truly awake for the first time I can remember. Awake and listening, listening for an endless time to these people who have saved my life. It's hard to listen. It's hard to stay awake.

A woman rushes into the room, a man not far behind her. The hunter. The woman sets a bucket next to me. What have I been throwing up? I have my answer right away because, as I wonder it, I am heaving again, and this time water and bile pour out of me. I'm throwing up fluids, remnants of the juice and broth they've methodically pumped into me. I feel as though I am dying for the second time.

"You're safe now," says the woman who gave me the bucket, Lara. "You're at Saint Francis." But three days ago I was in a dense wood, miles and miles from anywhere. I might have died there eventually, lost without food and water, miles from any town, if the hunters hadn't found me.

"They were hunting deer," she said. She said they almost hunted me. But instead, they carried me to their truck, because I was too weak and tired to walk much farther. They loaded me up like one of the animals they'd shot. They brought me to the shelter.

"Maybe I shoulda brought her to the hospital," the one called Frank says anxiously. "That was a nasty bruise on her cheek. But she was walking and talking just fine. . . ."

"It's OK, Frank," says the woman named Lara. "You did the right thing."

"You think," he starts, then again in a lowered voice: "You think another abuse case?"

"Probably. We've got it under control, though. You can stop checking up on her now," she says to him in a teasing voice. Through droopy eyelids I see her give him a quick kiss on the cheek before he walks away. This little gesture tells me everything. He didn't know where to bring me, so he brought me to the woman he loved. It

makes me happy and sad at the same time. I love someone, too.

My eyes start to droop.

"Abby," the woman called Lara says. There's a little tug
on my necklace. "It's Abby, right? Wake up, honey." I try
my hardest to look at her, but all I want to do is go back to
sleep. My upper lids are magnets to my lower. I am gone.

"Abby?" I hear. I see a lovely woman, a brown-haired
goddess, bent over my bed. It is Lara. I hadn't known
before that she was so beautiful.

My fault . . .

"Yes," I say, even though I know for certain now that
Abby isn't my name at all.

No one can know.

"How are you feeling?" the woman asks.

"OK," I say, even though I'm not OK; my insides are
twisted in pain and sadness.

Don't show it.

"Sweetheart," she says, and instead of sounding
patronizing, it sounds nice. "Do you remember me? You
came in a few days ago and have been in and out of it
ever since."

"I think so," I say. I do remember her bending over me
with the hunter beside her, telling me her name, telling
me everything is going to be OK. I remember sensing
that this woman is good.

"Honey, can you tell me your full name?"

I pause.

Don't tell.

I can't tell her my name. This one thought penetrates all the haze. I can't tell her my real last name because then she'll know who I am. Then she'll know I killed my family. The nausea overwhelms me again, and Lara watches as I relieve myself in the bucket that's still by my bed.

"It's Abby," I say when I'm finally finished. "Abby Jameson." It's not quite strong enough but I'm weak, too weak to think of something else.

"How old are you, Abby?" Lara asks.

"Eighteen," I say. It isn't true; I'm just over seventeen, but I can't tell her that. Eighteen is the age where you can do what you want. Eighteen is safe.

"I hate to put you through more than you've already dealt with," she continues, "but do you mind telling me what you were doing out in those woods? Judging by how weak you are, you must have been out there for a while."

"I don't know" is all I can say. There's a long silence. Then Lara stands up from where she's been sitting at the foot of the bed; something in her shifts, some pained look turns to stone, and now she's all business.

"This is my shelter, Abby. You're lucky you ended up here. Frank's a good man. We have a dedicated staff here, and it's women only. We're a Christian-based organization, and we're always short on beds; there are always people knocking on our door. Our guests are allowed to stay for thirty days. We give you all the resources you need for getting back on your feet, finding a job. This is, of course, if you don't have someone you can call, somewhere else you can go."

I shake my head. "I don't have a family," I say.

"Fine," she tells me. "The amount of time you seem to have spent on your own and the fact that you have no identification on your person would support that. In my experience, if you had someone looking for you, they would have found you by now. I'd turn you over to Social Services, but since you say you're eighteen"—she gives me a long look—"I'm entitled to leave you be. At least until I check into it. I'm going to be confirming your story for our records, of course. Protocol. Meanwhile, try to use this time to your benefit." I nod. I don't know why she is suddenly cold, but I am relieved that she doesn't seem interested in inquiring much further, and doubly relieved that I thought to give her a different name.

"Oh, Abby?" she says. "There's one other thing. We require all of our guests to see a consulting psychologist. Donations help pay for his work. The rest he does pro bono; and since it's something I firmly believe in, I tend to enforce it. You play by our rules, or you go. And in your case," she adds a little more gently, "it might be especially beneficial. He can see you for up to six months for free, even after you're not a guest here anymore. We'll give it a week or so, until your physical health has improved."

I don't say anything. I can't. I'm crying too hard, silent sobs that shatter my broken body. I've never felt so alone. Lara hands me a box of tissues, and with a light pat to my shoulder, she is gone.

CHAPTER FORTY-NINE
Thirteen Days After

There are Navajo prints on the walls of Dr. Tessler's office. The whole place is dimly lit and decorated with shelves of books, various Native American wall hangings, and frayed carpets—the kind that are supposed to look frayed, as though handcrafted. I imagine Dr. Tessler selecting these from a specialty store downtown, considering ambiance and how it will affect his patients, hoping people will think he's acquired these from some small village in the Southwest. Or maybe he has. I don't know. Maybe people aren't always pretending.

I gently ease my body, still aching, into a leather recliner, but there are a few different chairs to choose from. I like that about this place. I chose this one because it looks like it could swallow me whole, wrap its leather arms around me, and tuck me inside itself. I sink farther into the leather, pushing myself down in an effort to make it happen. I don't want to be here.

After Lara's hawk eyes, I prepared for more questions. I keep my answers simple: *My name is Abby Jameson. I was in the woods. I don't know how I got there. I don't remember anything else.*

Dr. Tessler listens patiently at first, taking notes. But then things get harder. He asks me questions—what happened to my family? Did something happen, something scary, before I went to the woods? Can I remember anything that might have been traumatic? Do I have a history of sexual abuse? I field these questions, bouncing them back like Ping-Pong balls, until the hour is nearly up and I am drenched in sweat, all over my body.

It's not long before the irony hits me: not long ago, I would have been as eager as Dr. Tessler is to know who I am. But now that I know, I have to hide it. I wonder if he can see the truth. I'm sure the guilt is everywhere, seeping out of my pores and lacing my lies. Even as I fight to stay calm, revulsion and something else, something that feels like despair, overwhelm me. *If he knew what a monster I am, what would he do? What would everyone do?* I am biting my lip, but tears come anyway. It's a relief when they do. All this time, I've tried not to think about what happened. I've felt storm clouds swirling under my rock exterior, and I've wanted to let them out—I have—but instead they stay under the surface, worsening. I've wanted to cry. I've felt like screaming. I've become a ticking bomb. I've ignored my own betrayals, let my guilt fester and worsen.

So now that tears have come, I can feel the pressure lessening just a bit.

I can see that Dr. Tessler likes the tears. They make me

somehow normal, someone he can wrap his head around. He is the kind of man who looks like a puppy — sincere and hopeful. He looks like he could be beaten down with a stick. He disgusts me. I watch him watching me as I snuffle into the tissue he's given me, and rage begins to consume me. Here is the man who could destroy me if he asks too many questions. And all the time he's destroying me, he will think he's helping.

Something tells me that I am not really mad at Dr. Tessler, that the uncontrollable anger I feel is really just anger I've felt all along, but somehow he's pushed the buttons that have given it freedom, but it's too hard to think that way and too easy to direct my rage at him. I've been not-thinking for days. He's made me think, and remember.

"I think we've made good progress for a first session," he says gently, and, when I don't respond he adds, "You're free to go now, Abby. I'll see you next week." I nod and exit his office, which is just a couple of blocks from Saint Francis. I'll need to think things over before next week. I'll need to be even more prepared for his probing questions.

He can't say anything, even if he suspects, I tell myself. It's confidential. But I know the truth; I'm just fooling myself. If Dr. Tessler knew what I'd done, he'd go to the police. I almost don't care; I wonder for a quick second if it would be a relief for someone to know, to see me for who I really am. To see the blood on my hands. But I can't; I just can't. I don't know what to do. I can't be here, hiding my secret, forever. But I'm still sick; I'm so weak. I don't know if I'm strong enough to survive on my own just yet. Tears are still streaking down my face, and I'm shivering even though there's barely a chill in the air. I see an alley toward the end of the block and head for it; it looks like it cuts all the way through. A shortcut. I don't want to be away from Saint Francis longer than I have to.

As soon as I enter the alley, I realize it's a mistake; whereas the sidewalks were lit by streetlamps, the alley is pitch-black. It's just after eight but dark enough back here to be three a.m. As my eyes begin to adjust, I notice that it's not just an alley at all: it must have been a back path into some small housing development. I turn back only to find that I can't see the road anymore; it's vanished entirely. I realize I must have lost track in my panic. I must have wandered down one of the other paths that stretch from where I stand like fingers, or spiderwebs, or a maze. I take a breath and turn, walking a few paces back toward the direction I think I came from.

Nothing looks familiar.

And then a familiar and irrational thought: I'm going to die out here.

I steady myself. I am not going to die out here. I will walk through this place until I see someone or hit a main road, and then I will ask for directions. I must be so close. No more than a half mile away.

But it looks dangerous back here.

I shouldn't be afraid. I don't need to be afraid. I push myself forward; I have no idea, no idea at all, how I became so lost. As I walk, I'm surrounded by trash, broken bottles, and leftover chicken bones sitting next to crumbling stoops. I've never really been out of the shelter until now. On the way to my session, when Lara walked me so carefully and told me I'd be OK getting back—after all, I'm eighteen—my mind was preoccupied with lies.

And then I see two figures on one of these urban stoops, and I am terrified. They watch me silently with glittering eyes; they wave cigarettes, the only evidence of light, with slender wrists. They are mistresses of the dark, so dark that I am nearly upon them before I see them. And after I do, I look straight ahead, too afraid to ask them where I am. Afraid of everything now. The alley is so small; I wonder if it is worse to pass them without saying something. But I do it anyway, quickening my step.

It's too late by the time I notice one long, bronze leg extending itself in front of me. I stumble, and I nearly fall before I catch myself. I try to walk on as if nothing happened, but they're laughing too loud and too long for just two people. It's a chorus behind me, half beautiful and half cruel.

I run for far too long, maybe more than half a mile, before I stop feeling the familiar sears of panic. Before I can think again. I don't know what I've wandered into—some sort of housing project. It hits me that I have no way out; that this is the worst place for me to be, that I can't ask for directions here.

But is this place any different from where I was with Sam? Am I any different from those girls on the stoop? No, surely not. I am thinking the way Addie thinks, not the way Abby would have thought. And now I'm both girls, both identities. Or neither girl, someone braver still. My fear is nothing.

It's as if this realization saves me, as if my fear had been sabotaging me, leading me deeper into the maze. Because as I turn left, relying on instinct and calmer than before, I see a dim haze of light far ahead. It doesn't matter what road it is. Any road will do. Any road with people or maybe a gas station where I can ask for directions. I walk straight ahead, quicker and more confidently now, and I'm only a few blocks away when I hear a voice beside me: "Hey, sexy."

I whip around; there's a figure next to me who hadn't been there just a second ago. He's about my age, and he's wearing a baseball cap pulled low over his eyes. But I'd recognize that build, that skin, anywhere. My heart turns to fire-ice.

Sam.

I am too afraid even to scream, but screaming wouldn't do me any good here anyway, so I run. But as I run, I realize I *am* screaming, kind of. A high-pitched squealing sound that isn't loud enough to get any attention, but I can't seem to get any louder.

"Wait!" I hear, then some muttering, then some other voices and then, louder: "That chick is *wacked,* yo." And still louder, in a shout so I can hear: "You hear me, girl? You *wacked.*"

I run and run. It's only a few blocks, but it may as well be miles.

I can't tell whether he's behind me.

I almost cry when I reach the street because I recognize it; there is Saint Francis on the corner, just twenty feet away.

I run without looking back.

And it is only now, only after relief washes over me in a tidal wave, after the onslaught of emotion lifts me outside of my body, that I can answer my own question.

I know. I know what happened to Katie that night. The memory is thick and rancid, and with it comes a final, unbearable pain.

Sam pushes me to the ground, and we start down the staircase on all fours, me in front and him behind. I am feeling my way down and am nearly there when I hear a shriek that doesn't belong to me. I am seized by it briefly, and I almost can't move because I'd know it anywhere. Katie is inside. And now, now I remember what she whispered to me once, her secret I'd dismissed as false, an attempt at showing off.

"Sometimes, Addie, I skip cheer camp and nap away the day, listen to music, do my own thing for a while, and Mama never knows the difference. She doesn't even know I'm home."

"Yeah, right. Where would you even go?"

"The attic, silly. Right behind all those old crates, on top of the ratty sofa in the corner."

"I hope you know you're using ratty literally, Katie. That's disgusting."

"Suit yourself. Just don't rat me out." Then she'd laughed at her joke, looking up at me teasingly.

"If you're always skipping out, Katie," I asked quietly, "how do you stay on cheer?"

"I'm just that good," she said with a wink. "It doesn't take much." And I felt revulsion fill my mouth and belly despite myself. Katie could flirt her way out of anything. Classes, cheer practice, extra chores around the house. She was that charming and, if I was honest, that sneaky.

And now I know for sure in the worst possible way that Katie hadn't been joking. I'm so close to the door I can almost touch it, but I turn anyway. Sam grabs for me again, but he misses this time, and I clamber back up the stairs toward the sound of the scream. Sam frantically yells for me from the bottom. When I reach the top of the staircase, it's louder, but the wall of flames that covered the doorframe to the attic before has now shot across the first few steps, forming a curtain of flames. Through it, I see her.

"Addie!" she screams. "Please, Addie!"

I crawl toward her and look for a way around it. There is none.

"Come through it!" I yell to her. "Or jump from up there." I motion toward the attic.

"I can't," she says. "I'm too scared."

"Don't be scared. Turn around, jump from the top. Or run through to me and I'll smother the flames."

"No." She is crying now. She reaches toward me. I try to reach for her, and I gather every tiny piece of strength from deep in my soul and I stay strong for her, because I need her more than anyone. She is the one person who fully understands me, who never asks more from me than what I am. I am reaching toward the flames because I want to pull her through to me since she won't do it herself. I am gasping and reaching when I see the wooden beam, a torch ablaze, hurtle from the rafters above her. I close my eyes because I know where it will land. And when I open them again, I see I was right; she is lying motionless and I can barely make out her eyes, wide and still, staring into mine.

I run from her. I am consumed by smoke and flames and

guilt and shame and horror until I can't tell them apart. Everything is crumbling; the stairs give way beneath my feet, and there is tremendous noise, as if from an earthquake. And when I wake up, there is an angel above me, stroking my cheek, and I can't remember a thing.

CHAPTER FIFTY

Sixteen Days After

I am a specter, haunting and haunted, living in an in-between land. But at least now I am living, instead of caught in a dream. Sometimes I think the dreamworld was easier; sometimes I even miss it. But then I look down at the scar that inches its way from my thumb and forefinger to my wrist, my painful reminder of the night I lost everything, and I accidentally catch sight of my hollow cheeks and sunken eyes in the mirror, and I know: the world I lived in with Sam was a beautiful fantasy, but it would have killed me in the end.

I slip in and out of the cracks at Saint Francis. I take everything in and give nothing back. I watch and hear. I never talk. Talking is damning, and my secrets well up in my chest and threaten to push out all the time. But the shelter isn't a purgatory for just me; *thirty days* hovers thick in the air like a death sentence. I can see an invisible hourglass hovering over everyone's heads. My own has fourteen grains of sand left. When I am tired of watching, I sketch furiously. Sketch and watch, watch and sketch. Anything not to think.

There are a few guests here, mostly younger girls — high-school dropouts and former crackheads and teenage moms, who keep the place filled with chatter as though there's a perpetual TV on in the background. But most of the women here are like me. Quiet, private. Not very talkative except for the pleases and the thank-yous. That's because there's no reason to form connections when no one's sticking around for very long anyway.

But I have extra motivation to stay silent: it's impossible to feel safe here. Each morning, I wake up wondering if today someone will recognize me. If today I will see an old neighbor, or a friend of my mother's, some kind-hearted soccer mom who's willing to drive an hour from home to volunteer at the Saint Francis soup kitchen. Every day I wake up wondering if it's my last day of freedom.

And then there's Sam. I miss him and fear him all at once. I know by now that the boy in the alley couldn't have been Sam; Sam never spoke like that, and he would have shown up at Saint Francis by now, looking for me. I know that, but I am still afraid.

I see Sam now just as clearly as I see myself; I hate him and I fear him so much that I wake up screaming in terror from the nightmares in which he's pursuing me. But despite it all, I still love him. I hate myself for loving him. In my mind, I list the facts I've pieced together from memory:

—Sam was a drug addict.

—Sam traded my body for drugs.

—Sam knew the truth about my family and the night they died.

—Sam lied to me. Everything he said was a lie.

—We did not live in a cave-palace. The place we lived in was filthy and cold, maybe one of the hundreds of abandoned mines that litter the forests here.

Then why do I miss him? I do. I miss him. I miss the way he'd stroked my hair until I fell asleep. I miss his stories, and his brilliance, and his long laugh. Maybe part of me, in that alley, wanted it to be him.

Hey, sexy.

The beat of footsteps.

Being pursued.

Being caught. Wrapped in his arms. Taken with no choice.

But I am afraid of him. I am afraid of how much I miss him. I am afraid of the box of letters I keep hidden under my bed, letters I've written to him with the half intention of sending, if only I knew where. I'm glad I don't know where. I'm glad that no matter how many hours I've spent scouring the Internet on the shelter's computer, I've found nothing about him or the liquor-store robbery. Maybe Sam wasn't his real name. Maybe he lied about that, too.

I'm glad he's never there, hovering outside Saint Francis ringing the doorbell over and over and thumping his fist on the door, begging for someone to let him in, like so many of the women's former lovers. I'm glad every day that I don't see him on our stoop, but I'm also disappointed. Because he hooked me in the way the drugs hooked him. And now I don't trust myself not to go back. I don't know where he is, but I know he's close. I can feel his presence the same way I felt Katie speaking to me, telling me the truth about things, through time and space and delirium and hallucinations. I am torn between a sickening desire for Sam and a terrible revulsion. I know what I'm feeling is wrong, very wrong. My weakness fills me with self-loathing.

There's something else I found on the Internet:

July 10. Police have ruled out arson as a probable cause for the July 8 fire at the James residence on Orchard Lane. Officials state that the fire originated in the master bedroom, where a candle reacted with flammable materials to cause a blaze intense enough to buckle floor supports.

"This was no ordinary house fire," said Eric Davies, chief of police. "The house literally caved in on itself. The blaze was highly intense; our firefighters couldn't even get close to it."

Investigators have stated that due to the extreme temperatures and the color of the flames, it is likely that the collapsed floor materials ignited with paint thinners and turpentine, both of which were known to be stored in the family's basement, according to Al Reuter, a neighbor. Such materials, when burned, can reach the extreme temperatures necessary to reduce a home and its inhabitants to ash.

"I filled in with Justin, you know, on odd jobs here and there," said Reuter, referring to Justin James. "There was all kinds of stuff down there. Paint thinners, fertilizer, you name it. Justin was like that, always prepared for any job that might come up. There was tons of stuff. Tons of it. We never thought twice about it. You never think of stuff like this happening."

All four members of the James family are believed to have been home at the time of the incident, though they are currently filed as missing persons with the county police department. An official report will be released on Thursday.

I try hard not to think about it. But it's there, all the time, a hand pressed against my chest, suffocating my heart until I'm deader than they think I am, because not even a soul remains. All of my grief is not enough. Sometimes I wonder, when I sit on the long steel bench at mealtime, or when I wait in line for an open shower stall, how many of these women are like me — which ones are running from something, hearts beating from anxious adrenaline, and which ones are just stuck somewhere in

inertia, passing the time until they pass the time somewhere else. It's not so easy to tell. Everyone watches one
another, but this is what I see:

I see Myra, the obese woman who speaks to her belly
and clutches her back when she walks, hoping everyone
will think she's pregnant. I see the way Myra skips meals.
I see her trot back to her room at night, and because I
watch very closely, I know where she keeps her stash of
candy. I even know how much she eats: seven king-size
Hershey bars per night.

I see Lulu, a scrawny kid, maybe fourteen, who cocks
her fingers in the shape of a pistol and gnashes her teeth
together if you look her way. I see her stuff things in
her pockets when she thinks no one's watching: a cheap
plastic bracelet, a brownie from lunch, a postcard of
Las Vegas. And I see the way she hugs her drug-addled
mother when she bothers to visit. I see the way she slips
these treasures from her own palm into her mother's
pockets. I made a sketch last week, one night I couldn't
sleep. I made it extra-beautiful with lots of detail. It was
a sketch of the ocean, with a little beach hut off to the
side and a girl playing in the waves. The next morning, it
was stolen, but it was OK. I'd wanted her to have it.

And there are others. Others more like me who went
to bed one day and woke up somewhere else entirely.
Girls whose worlds changed in an instant because of a
mistake, or an accident, or a bad decision they thought

they could control until they found out they were horribly, grossly wrong. There are several drug addicts whose
jittery mannerisms remind me of Sam. I try not to notice.

What strikes me most profoundly in all my watching
and waiting is that I'm not very different from most of
the people here at all. Less than a year ago, I had a good
life: a family who cared, books and clothes even though
we weren't rich, and always plenty of food. Now I am
here. And all it took was one mistake to go from being
who I *was* to who I *am*. All in the flicker of a candle.
And I can't help but wonder, How many people here
would say the same thing happened to them? If only
someone told us all when we were little how easy it is
to fall. How no one at all belongs at the bottom — it's
just unfortunate luck, a bad choice made in a minute or
less. We think we're different, we're privileged, that those
people are down here for a reason. But now I know the
truth: they're not. It's just chaos, madness, accident, luck.

Even when I was with Sam, though, there was this
idea that we were somehow different, or better. He made
me believe we were destined for each other; that we
were smarter and more in love and *chosen*. Chosen for
greatness. If he were ever to find me here, he'd clasp my
hands in his, and even as track marks ran up and down
his forearms, he'd look around and laugh. And he'd say in
a gravelly voice, "What are you doing here, *mija*, with all
of these messed-up people? You don't belong here; you

belong with me." And the worst part is, I'd go. I'd follow his skeleton frame out of there and never look back. I'd follow him and live in a situation far worse than this, all the while make-believing that he and I were above all of that. And I'd look the other way when he indulged his habits, and then maybe the day would come when he'd get me hooked on more than just him. I'd follow Sam all the way to the grave. That's why I'm afraid of him. It would be my second grave. The whole world believes I'm dead, but I won't get there Sam's way, on a chariot of arrogance and obsession.

CHAPTER FIFTY-ONE

Twenty Days After

"I can't remember," I say, but I am lying. I remember everything.

"Try," Dr. Tessler says. "The memories are there, somewhere inside of you." I look at him then and he looks at me back and I see he's so painfully sincere.

I read once that there are hundreds of emotions that can translate themselves to the human eyes. I think this as I look into Dr. Tessler's brown orbs, which speak of all the ways he wants to fix me, as though I'm a puzzle he can reassemble if he only tries hard enough. And I remember my mother's eyes the way I always seem to think of them now: their warmth as she smiled at me on Sundays, flipping pancakes on the stove, extra butter and one of them cut in an *A* for *Addison*. Her eyes spoke of love, contentment, happiness. Emotions that seem so inconceivably distant now.

I remember Katie's wicked grin the first day she ever snuck out, scaling the tree next to our roof and hopping into the idling car below. She'd turned to me and winked, and I'd looked back at her, silently pleading with her to ask me along, knowing she never would, that in some ways I'd always just be alone. Even in the dim light of the street lamp, I could see it in her eyes: nervous abandon, pride, excitement, glee. Feelings that had everything to do with the parts of her life I couldn't share. And when she returned home that night and kissed me on the cheek, her breath hot with gin, her eyes radiated a soft, muddled kind of peace.

The eyes can say so much more than words.

I remember the night of the fire. My mother's eyes glowed amber in the reflection of the flames; they were pleading, frightened. My father's eyes shone with resignation. Katie's were worse. In them lay some emotion: maybe part regret, but also something more. Her eyes screamed awareness of the whole life she'd never see.

But of course I can't tell any of this to Dr. Tessler. I can't tell him because then *my* life—the only thing that remains of all of this—will vanish as easily as theirs did. I don't know why I want to live, but I do. And that fact is maybe even uglier than everything I've done to get here. It fills me with disgust. But I can't tell Dr. Tessler who I am.

Because I am a murderer.

I wear my family's blood like an impenetrable coat of armor. I betrayed them. I am a part of the very thing I've spent months fearing. I am Circle Nine. I am surprised Dr. Tessler can't see it for himself. He will return home tonight to his empty apartment, or maybe even to a loving family. He will settle back into his armchair, a replica of the one he keeps in his office, and reflect on my case. He'll sip a cup of coffee or a glass of whiskey, unwind from his long day. And he'll think, Maybe I can really get through to her. I hope I can. She's so young. . . . And later, he'll fall asleep easily, clearheaded and optimistic. Certain that somehow, some way, he can fix me.

And all the while I will sit on my cot at Saint Francis House, and for me it will all be real and so excruciating that I will, probably, question for the millionth time whether I really do want to go on alone or whether I should end it all now. After all, I think, even if I keep fighting, what's the point? Aren't I already condemned? But like the many times before, I will recognize that tiny glimmer in me that wants something more from life. What happened will still be true. I will still be responsible for all these deaths. I will still be without my family and without Sam, whom I still—despite everything— can't help but love. It's not an interesting case but a life—my life—and the lives I destroyed. I know in my gut that what I feel is beyond repair. And I know if I stay here and let this doctor pick apart my brain, the things he'll inevitably find will only make things worse.

I have to leave. I don't have much time.

"Abby?" I look up quickly. "Abby," he says again, and, as though he can read my thoughts: "What about Sam? Can you tell me about him?"

Sam. The name is a bullet through my chest. Sam's name did not come up in my previous sessions; I'd thought he, at least, would be easy to hide.

"I don't know who you mean," I say. The doctor peers at me closely. He knows I'm lying.

"Sam," he says. "According to the social worker from Saint Francis, you were repeating the name in your sleep."

"I don't know," I tell him. "I don't remember any Sam."

We sit in silence for ten minutes.

"You should know that Lara's run a background check," says Dr. Tessler seriously. "There are no missing persons reports filed under Abby Jameson." He pauses, as though choosing his words carefully. "We need your memories, Abby. There may be something that can help you if you're willing to try it. Hypnosis." He says it carefully, gauging my reaction. "Many people who suffer from what you're experiencing can easily enter hypnotic states." He forms his fingers into a little steeple in front of his chest. "Consider it. It could be very helpful." His words sound like a threat, but I nod anyway.

"It's noon, then," he says, as if it wouldn't have been noon otherwise. "Hang in there, Abby. I'll see you next week. You can call me anytime before that if there's anything at all you'd like to talk about." I nod, pushing myself out of the recliner I've come to hate. My time here is running out.

"An interesting book." His voice stops me just as I've

reached the door. "What did you think of it?" I swivel at this; I'm caught off-guard. Dr. Tessler has an odd, curious look on his face, as though I've surprised him somehow. At first I don't know what he's talking about, but then I remember; the *Inferno* is jutting from the pocket of my jacket, its bulky form halfway exposed. I don't know why I still carry it around. I guess because it's the one thing I still have left from my time with Sam.

"I'm not sure," I say carefully, even as my heart begins its instinctive race. "It's frightening."

"Yes," he agrees. "But necessarily so, wouldn't you agree? In the way it fits with the whole, I mean. Have you read the rest?"

"The rest?" Now it's me who is surprised.

"Oh, yes," he says. "You really ought to. The *Purgatorio* and the *Paradisus*. The *Inferno* is the most famous, of course; but it's only the beginning." I see that he is getting animated, as though this is a subject that interests him, but I don't mind because I am interested, too.

Only the beginning.

"It's all about the soul's ascent to heaven," Dr. Tessler continues, "starting in the bowels of hell and working its way up. At least that's it in very simple terms. It's really quite interesting; you should give it a look. A monster of a book, though," he says with a laugh. "I don't blame you if you don't. I only dug through it under threat of a failing grade, way back when, in college."

"OK," I tell him, forcing a casual tone. "Maybe I'll check it out." I can feel the warm flush spreading to my face, so I turn quickly, striding out the door before he has a chance to see how his words have affected me. *The soul's ascent to heaven.* So the story didn't end in hell at all; there's more to it. Something about knowing this makes me feel lighter, justifies my will to survive. All this time I've felt guilty for wanting to go on, but maybe survival is OK. I think about it all the way home, and it stays with me into the night, a tiny spark of hope embedded in my heart.

CHAPTER FIFTY-TWO

Twenty-Two Days After

I am on the streets, technically the sidewalk, crunched up next to a set of stone stairs. I am supposed to be looking for a job; instead, I am begging. Because of my health, I have not had to go on mandatory job searches before today.

Now I pull my baseball cap low over my face, a cap I borrowed from a girl named Thed, short for Theodora, for the afternoon. My body almost doesn't matter; by now it is a stranger's body. But I wear one of Thed's tight wife-beaters to show off my bones. It makes me look as skinny as I am. I feel naked, but it is so hot in this early-summer sun that I am grateful in a way. I sweat. I stare down at my sidewalk. It is the easiest way of making money. I've heard stories of people getting rich this way. So I'm doing it, even though there's a risk. But I've seen myself in the mirror. I think I look different enough now, so skinny, like one of those girls on the talk shows and nothing like myself. *Keep your head down. No one will recognize you. You could be anyone.*

I have eight days left at Saint Francis. Eight days to make enough money here on the sidewalk to get me far, far away, because after what happened with Sam, and after Dr. Tessler started asking me all kinds of questions I couldn't answer, I decided for sure that I have to get far away from here. I am worried that eight days isn't enough time. I'm worried it's too much, that someone will figure out who I am—*Addison James*—before then. It's the first time since I got here that I've let myself really acknowledge the name, connect it to myself. It feels like something dangerous. As if everyone can hear me whisper it privately in my head.

I know from Google maps that Saint Francis is about an hour by car from where I used to live, on the opposite end of the woods. I've been safe for now, or maybe just lucky, but an hour is not distant enough from my past. I won't get a job here, because I won't be staying here much longer. This time next week, I'll be gone.

I have been actively not-thinking about my family all day, but they maul my thoughts with their presence. They're with me all the time now. It is why I am sketching, even sitting here, sketching and begging. In my jacket pocket now is the *Purgatorio,* the book Dr. Tessler told me about, the one that comes after the *Inferno.* I took it from a bookstore yesterday, but I didn't steal it— I made a swap. I left my old copy of Sam's book in its place. The *Inferno* may have been beat up, but it was more than an even trade. It was hard to give it up. I can't read *Purgatorio* yet, though; I don't know what stops me, but for now it sits there, in my pocket, untouched—waiting for another day. Maybe a day when my thoughts are free and not constantly with my family, playing and replaying that horrible night. I wonder if that day will ever come.

I let one sliver of comforting thought cross my mind again and again: everyone thinks I am dead. All that time I was dreaming up my own world with Sam, I was dead in this world, in Circle Nine. That is why no one has searched for me. The fact that I am believed to be dead is why I am still alive, allowed to wander free in this world. Then the familiar sliver of horror: if someone recognizes me, someone I used to know, it's all over. I don't think about the other things I read in the clippings I have found. I don't think about them all afternoon.

Instead I think, *If I can make some money, I will be gone.* I've been sitting here for four hours and I'm only four hours away from heading back to Saint Francis for dinner, and I've so far made only twenty-five cents. *What am I doing wrong?* I even brought my sketches to sell, so it's not as though I'm just asking for money; I have something to give in return. I sold one sketch, the one that made me twenty-five cents, to a blind man. He wandered up with his dog, and when he figured out there was a me beside him, he asked what I was doing on the sidewalk all alone. I told him I was homeless — it's almost the truth, anyway — and the old man's eyes teared up and he reached into his pocket and I thought I was made — that I could go home and buy a bus ticket right away—but he only pulled out a quarter and dropped it into my palm. At the last minute, I reached over and tore off one of my sketches to give him. It ripped partway because I was too quick to tear, but he won't be able to look at it anyway, so I'm not sure it even matters.

"Lovely!" he muttered, holding it up in front of his unseeing face. "I'm going to hang it in my kitchen." And then he and his dog shuffled away, and now I'm sitting here wondering what else is hanging in the blind man's kitchen. The sketch he took was of Myra from the shelter. Now he'll have this in addition to the poems from one man on the corner opposite and maybe the dirty license plates I've seen others sell. Anything is treasure here. Anything is worth money. And anyway, it isn't the stuff that's being sold that actually *sells*. It's me. It's us. The stuff is just so people won't feel like we're being paid to take naps all day.

But some people give the nappers money, too.

Almost no one gives me money.

I imagine it's because they can see my guilt written in my posture, in the way I grimace-smile, on the scar snaking up my right forearm. They look down at me as they go by. Most pretend not to, flicking their eyes over at the last second or slowing their steps to stare out of their periphery, but some stare openly. I fight the urge to stare back. I'm not supposed to. I've seen how others do things. And I won't let anyone see my face, just in case.

In the next four hours:

A man wearing a blue polo shirt and khaki pants leers down at me, asks, "What are your rates, sweetheart?" I don't answer him. It's an easy way to make money—I know that. But I can't. It makes me think of Sid. It makes my heart shrink into a cold, hard pebble. I ignore him until he walks away in a cloud of swearwords, looking all around and over his shoulders to see if anyone noticed.

A little boy walks by, maybe four years old, clutching his mother with one hand and waving around a half-eaten peanut-butter sandwich in the other. His head is about as high as mine is, sitting here. Maybe a little higher. He is wearing green overalls and saddle shoes and a cap like mine. He's chewing, but he stops all of a sudden and thrusts the sandwich at me. I take it instinctively. Food isn't what I need, at least right now, but his gesture is so natural and sweet that I respond without even thinking. He turns as they keep walking, watching to see if I've taken a bite, and I do take one, and I smile my hard pebble-grimace, and he waves, and his mother never notices anything, and my eyes fill up just a little because she may never know this—this pure, beautiful thing—about her son. And I bet she'd be proud if she knew.

A dog stops and sniffs at me and lifts his leg to pee, but then his owner, a middle-aged woman, jerks him away and says, "No!" sharply. Then she blushes a little and says, "Sorry" with a little smile and places some change on the ground in front of me. She hurries off before I can thank her, and her shoulders are all hunched over and she walks fast like she's terrified and anxious all at the same time. I wonder if she's afraid of something like I am—if that's how I move, too.

I only make a dollar twenty-five for the whole day. Even if I could sit out here for another thirty days, it wouldn't be enough to get anywhere. The day has somehow made my need to get away, to start over, even more urgent. I will need to think of something else, because a dollar twenty-five is not nearly enough to buy my freedom.

I see a lot of things, though—things that make it worth it. Some beauty and a little filth, like the leering man, but more beauty than filth. And it's obvious all of a sudden that everything's all mixed up: you can't guard yourself entirely from one thing or another because anywhere you are, there's good and bad jumbled up like a huge casserole or like trail mix (I think of these things because I am suddenly very hungry), and you can never just have good *or* bad, one or the other. They're both there, all the time, in Circle Nine or in my head or probably anywhere else, at least while we're alive. I'm still alive. I know that now. I am not Addie anymore; too many people and things that made me Addie are now gone forever. And I never was Abby; she was something imaginary, some piece of fiction that Sam and I created. But I am here, and I am OK, even though I'm not exactly sure who I've become. And all of a sudden I want to see all the things I was shielding myself from when I was in the woods.

But I do hope that wherever Katie and my parents are, somewhere far away from this world, it's only good.

CHAPTER FIFTY-THREE

Twenty-seven Days After

Dr. Tessler adjusts his glasses and clears his throat in a way I can't stand. I am keyed up, jittery in anticipation of what he might say to me today, or what he might make me say. He is cunning; I know that now. I know his cunning is maybe what makes him good at what he does, and I can see that I am right from all the degrees on his walls, from the framed awards he must have received over the course of his many years of doing what he does, which is to open up people's minds and put them back together.

Which is to make me remember, make me feel all these things I don't want to feel, especially in front of him.

Which is why I hate him.

But instead of asking me questions, he folds his hands over his plaid shirt, which tugs apart a little at the belly, and speaks to me with complete directness for maybe the first time. This is my third session. I have three days left at Saint Francis.

"Abby," he says, "today I just want you to listen. I'll do all the talking. You can ask me as many questions as you like when I am finished. I think you'll enjoy asking the questions this time." He smiles a little at this,

his attempt at humor, before continuing. "It seems like you have no trouble remembering what it was like for you out there in the woods, but you seem to be having a little bit of difficulty remembering what happened just before you found yourself there. Now, I don't know if this is subconscious or conscious." At this I feel my face turning hot, but I don't say anything. I won't. "It may possibly be your psyche's way of telling you that you're not ready to confront whatever happened to you head-on. But it'll undoubtedly come out in time, particularly as you become adjusted to your new environment and as you begin to feel comfortable during our sessions." I nod. I can tell he knows I've been hiding something; I am growing more and more uncomfortable. But he said I didn't have to talk, so I don't.

"At any rate, I am aware that you'll soon be leaving Saint Francis, and we both know that means you're not required to see me anymore, but I hope you'll consider coming voluntarily. I think I can help you, Abby. I think you'll benefit from our relationship. I can help you deal with what's already happened to you, and I can help you transition." He stops here, waiting for my reaction. He's right: I will be leaving Saint Francis soon. And I'll be leaving Vermont, too, for good. I am certain of it, because now I have a plan. I am only here, going through the motions, because I have to. I have to leave quietly when my time is up. I have to avoid attracting suspicion.

"OK," I say, meaning *I understand,* but he takes it for something more positive than what it was meant to be and hurries forward.

"Good," he says, visibly pleased. "I think it will very much help you to understand the full nature of what you've experienced. It's important that you know you're not the only one who's gone through this. And that you shouldn't fear it happening again." *Happening again.* That wasn't something I had thought of. I had thought of it in the most superficial sense—in the idea of *Sam* happening to me again—but I'd never considered everything else happening again: the lies I told myself, the world I lived in. Going crazy. That's what it was. I went crazy. It was the obvious thing that should have occurred to me, and I feel foolish that it never did.

"I believe," says Dr. Tessler, "that you experienced a disorder called dissociative fugue. It's not that common, but it's much, much more common in women than in men. It typically involves some sort of journey from your home to elsewhere, which is the fugue part of it, and you seem to fit this criteria. And it often involves complete amnesia for its duration, anywhere from a couple of hours to many months. In your case it would have been about two or three months, from what we can tell from your story and your physical state, *and*"—he pauses here, and I can tell he's about to say something that he thinks will interest me, and he's probably right because I am completely and utterly absorbed despite myself—"and perhaps most interesting, it's characterized by a loss of one's own identity, *and*, in some very rare cases, the individual actually adopts an entirely new identity." He stops, taking a breath and looking at me carefully. I don't know what to feel. It's my situation. It is somehow a relief to know there's a label for it—that it's something worth labeling, something other people have gone through—but there's still one question.

"How do people get this . . . disorder?" I ask quietly.

"That's the thing," says Dr. Tessler, leaning forward in his chair. "That's actually the part of the puzzle that's missing for you. It's *always* triggered by some traumatic event. A lot of soldiers get it as a result of the things they see in battle. And sometimes people get it as a result of abuse—typically sexual abuse—which is why I asked you about that in one of our other sessions. But many people get it because something sudden and horrible happens to them—something so horrible their minds can't deal with it and they disconnect, or disassociate, entirely. The whole thing can happen in perfectly healthy individuals, not as a result of drug use or any other psychological disorders, and you're both clean and otherwise healthy. So like I said," he tells me quietly, peering at me intently from behind his spectacles, "there is some part of your puzzle that must be missing. I think if we can only bring it to the surface, you'll make a lot of progress. I hope we can work on it together. Whatever it is, Abby, this is a safe place."

I am only half listening as he continues telling me the ins and outs of this thing I have—dissociative fugue—which sounds like something slimy and infested. He knows. He knows for sure that I'm hiding something. Something so big and so horrible that it pushed me out of my mind for a while and warped me forever. I wish I could tell him what I did that night. I wish I could work on it and get better. I wish I could let him help me. But even as I'm wishing these things, I feel the same suffocating guilt for even wanting to get better when my family is gone. They didn't get another chance; they didn't get to do anything over. I will never, ever tell him. I will live with my secret forever.

CHAPTER FIFTY-FOUR

Thirty Days After

This is what should have happened next. This is the way I dreamed it would happen, over and over. I wish it could have been this way.

It's there, just like I remember it. I walk through the heavy iron gate, ironically the gate to a cemetery, past tiny clusters of mourners, and I have no trouble at all finding what I'm looking for; the tree is one year older than before, but I imagine the extra year only adds to its grace and beauty. It is gnarled, elegant. Its long branches bow toward the ground, nearly sweeping the frosty grass with their fingertips. It's nearly barren now, of course, in preparation for Vermont's cold winter. Even without the protection of most of its leaves, it's still majestic, still welcoming. I climb to the top and find the spot, our spot, where we used to squeeze in together and hide from the world, and trace our initials with my thumb. Still there, even after so many months of neglect. I used to like to imagine all the history this tree has seen, never realizing that someday we — my sister and me — would be just another blip in its century-long cycle. I sit here for a while, thinking of my parents, then when I can no longer keep them at bay, I allow my mind to train itself on my memories of Katie. She's the reason I need to be here.

"I'm so sorry, Katie," I whisper. Saying it out loud makes it feel somehow trivial and less of an apology, so I say it in my head—everything I've wanted to tell her since it happened. I sit in our old spot in our tree and tell my sister how sorry I am. I tell her how much I loved her, and how she saved my life back then, and again now, because the memories of how happy I was when I had her have given me reason to go on in spite of everything that's happened since.

When I finish, hours have gone by. I am drained and shaken, sedated and luminous, as if my parts have divided and are floating around me instead of sticking to me, as they should. Finally, I scramble back to the ground. My fingers unclasp my necklace without communicating with my brain or heart.

In my mind, I slip the gold necklace around her neck.

I want you to have it forever, I think at her. It means courage to exist in an imperfect world.

I push the necklace under the soil beneath the tree.

Abby, it reads, its letters partially obscured by earth and grass. My gift from her, it named me when I didn't know who I was. It brought me back to who I was supposed to be.

CHAPTER FIFTY-FIVE

Thirty Days After

But instead, this is what happened the day after my session with Dr. Tessler. I told myself it was how it had to be.

During job-search hours, I walked straight, head bent and shoulders hunched, baseball cap in place, for at least a mile. I walked until I felt far enough away. I went into a gas station and asked where the nearest pawnshop was. There is always a pawnshop, no matter where you are.

I walked back in the direction I came, asking for directions twice more before I found it. I stopped in front of it: a nondescript brick building, sandwiched between two other buildings, with a cheap yellow awning: *Buy, Sell, or Trade!* it read, as if everyone to walk in there wouldn't leave with a heavy heart.

I opened the door and stepped inside. I approached the counter. A line. I waited two or three minutes. A woman with a porcelain tea set: twenty dollars. Then me. Facing a register boy, too young to work in this business, with a face full of acne.

My fingers unclasp my necklace without communicating with my brain or heart.

"Seventy," the boy said.

"That's not right." My fingers were shaking. "I need at least three hundred. Look—it's twenty-four-karat gold. And there's a diamond." My voice had risen a few octaves. I'd sounded desperate. The boy sighed, not a real sigh, but a bargaining sigh. One that said, *I'll meet you somewhere in the middle. You know it; I know it.* He pulled out a magnifying glass from below the desk and pretended to look closer at the stamp on the necklace. I turned away.

"Not that many people will want to buy it," he said. "It says *Abby*. There's not that many people named Abby who wander in here."

"I know," I hissed. There were tears.

"All right, all right," he said, palms up. "One twenty-five, since there's a diamond. That's the best I can do."

I nodded. And then it was done.

CHAPTER FIFTY-SIX

Thirty Days After

I wish I had done it the other way: spoken to my sister, told her how sorry I am. Grieved my family the way I want to—the way I would if I weren't forever twisted, defunct. Maybe even let Dr. Tessler try to fix me.

But instead, I am on a bus, with nothing but my old clothes and the book I've taken, moving away from my past at fifty-five miles per hour. I won't read the book just yet. Instead I will allow myself to stay where I have become comfortable, just me alone with all the things I am feeling below the surface, afraid to rise out of it or sink farther down. I still can't let the feelings out, or I will fall apart, splintering into millions of pieces. Maybe I'll never be able to let them out. And maybe the *Purgatorio* will ever remain tucked under one arm, unopened. After all, how can I know just now what will happen, who I will become? I have ten hours ahead of me before my ticket's up, and then I'll have to find another way. But I will—I will always find some other way.

Maybe one day, I'll have the life I left behind. Maybe I'll open an art studio in California, sketch portraits by the waves, live in a modest little house and walk barefoot to work, use the one thing I'm good at to take me somewhere better. Maybe I won't be Abby or Addie there, but someone else entirely, someone bold and capable and strong.

Maybe I'll turn into someone I can be proud of, someday.

Maybe someday, I'll fall in love again.

Maybe I'll have a family. And if I do, I will open my heart to them without fear for myself. I will teach them to give back to the world. I'll show them how loved they are and I'll live in every moment of all of the pain that comes along with loving.

I promise myself that I'll do all of these things someday.

One thing: after this, no more hiding. I'll never hide again.

But for now, I'll just sit on this bus, and I'll watch the Vermont mountains rush by, and I'll dream.

ACKNOWLEDGMENTS

I am so grateful to those who lent me support of all kinds as I completed this book, and to the people who were there to encourage me as a developing writer long before the idea for this novel was conceived: Hilary Van Dusen, Josh Adams and Tracey Adams, Tor Seidler, Jackie Resnick, Suzanne LaFleur, Terence Heltzel, Alex Heltzel, Professor Katherine Tillman, Bob Jones, and especially, Patrick Chan.